A ROSE
IN ROATAN

A Novel

Nancy Kolodzie
and
Georges Benay

A Rose in Roatan

ISBN: 978-1-970157-74-1

Story Merchant Books
400 S. Burnside Avenue #11B
Los Angeles, CA 90036
www.storymerchantbooks.com

This is a work of fiction. Names, characters, businesses, places, events and incidents are either the products of the author's imagination or used in a fictitious manner. Any resemblance to actual persons, living or dead, or actual events is purely coincidental.

Book Interior and E-book Design: Amit Dey (amitdey2528@gmail.com)
Cover Design: Tatiana Villa

First Printing Edition 2025

*For my parents, Jean and Edward,
who taught me patience, kindness, and
exemplified The Golden Rule.*

In memory of Rachel and Elias Benay

"If you enjoy the fragrance of the rose, you must accept the thorns which it bears."

—William C. Bryant

TO OUR READERS

If you loved this story, *A Rose in Roatan*,
please write a telling review
on Amazon.

—Nancy Kolodzie and Georges Benay

ACKNOWLEDGEMENTS

I was inspired to tell this story after a trip to Roatan with my life partner, Georges, who, at that time, happened to be a writer without a story. Together we penned *A Rose in Roatan*, which was a journey in itself. It was only after we completed the project that I realized certain segments of this story resided in my mind long before a single word had been written.

I owe a special thanks to my co-author and life partner, Georges, who helped me make good use of some deeply buried emotions and inspired me to find my voice.

Mental illness touched my life even before I understood what it was. Our wish is to raise awareness of mental illness and invoke compassion and understanding.

—Nancy Kolodzie

My soulmate, Nancy, provided the initial spark for this novel. Her personal experience served as our guiding light in this extraordinary journey. I'm a believer in the human capacity to imagine beyond the thinkable. The genesis of a book can take many turns. Some ideas come spontaneously. Others vanish from the mind, only to come roaring back in the middle of the night in moments of intense subconscious creativity. Some stories are told to entertain. Others, to teach or to inform. Yet, stories that evoke empathy, compassion, or just a strong emotional connection seem to stick longer in our mind.

While writing is mostly a solitary task, the conversion of a manuscript into a book requires teamwork.

We are especially grateful to Ken Atchity at Story Merchant, who immediately took a liking for the novel, and was instrumental in getting the book onto the shelves of bookstores.

Sam Skelton and Charlotte Drummond deserve a special debt of gratitude for their excellent Launch Analysis. Their comments and observations were a great source of inspiration and helped us make the novel a much better read. They opened our eyes to so many possible avenues for the storyline.

A special thanks to Yvette Szmidt, Catherine Booth, and Nick Kolodzie, who took the time to read and provide insightful suggestions, encouragements, and comments on the very first draft of the novel. Their initial observations contributed to the evolution of the narrative up to the last page.

Many thanks, too, to our copyeditor and editors, Christine Dixon, Sam Skelton, and Charlotte Drummond who somehow managed to produce a coherent piece of work out of a rough manuscript. Additionally, thanks to Tatiana Villa for the wonderful book cover design—without forgetting all the folks who had a hand one way or another in the production of this book.

Many thanks to you all.

Be patient and kind to one another. You never know what a person is truly going through.

PROLOGUE

The Roatan Island Tribune

Woman Pulled from the Water at Little French Key

ROATAN—*Little French Key is usually a popular and safe place to scuba dive or snorkel, but caution should be exercised in the beach area where strong undercurrents can be treacherous.*

A woman was carried out of the water by a man at Little French Key earlier this week. The woman was without vital signs when paramedics arrived and administered first aid.

The Roatan Paramedic Service and police said the woman, who is currently in critical condition, was transported by water ambulance to a nearby health centre.

Circumstances are not clear as to why the woman was snorkeling in a clearly marked unsafe area. Roatan Police are investigating the matter which, according to the officer in charge, is standard procedure. Although little is known as to how the drowning incident occurred, investigators said they are treating it as an accident.

"At first, I saw a whole bunch of people running around screaming. I went to check what was happening and saw a man giving CPR to an unconscious woman. The whole thing was quite scary. I mean, it's usually so safe around here," said Cathy, a tourist present at the time.

Visitors at Little French Key are being reminded to put safety first while in the water. The Roatan Police Department reminds swimmers, snorkelers, and scuba divers to stay clear of the areas on the beach deemed unsafe. Additional warning signs will be posted in the high-risk areas.

When I first read this news article, I understood that things are not always what they seem. People have secrets. It is an unfortunate fact but a universal truth nonetheless. Most secrets are kept out of fear—fear of being tagged as a fraud (the impostor complex), fear of being the guilty one, fear of rejection, and fear of disappointing, among others. Indeed, fears and secrets go hand in hand. And fear can sometimes lead to unsavoury consequences.

But over the course of a gut-wrenching series of incidents, I eventually learned that not all secrets are borne out of fear. Still, they are not without pain and anguish. These are secrets of the mind, but more about that later.

The story I am about to tell you took place on a tiny island off the coast of Honduras. My story is not unique, in that it is also about a sequence of events and revelations, and the people that are entangled in this web. Was it coincidence or fate that brought us together in the same place at the same time? When I look back at what happened, I am left with a deep sense of bewilderment. And the only thing that I'm certain of is that what took place on that island had a profound effect on our lives.

As I read the news article for the second time, I came to the realization that there was no conceivable definitive ending possible to my story. Just a happy pause to a long cycle of slow progress. No one has yet been able to fully unravel the secrets of the mind. That's the conundrum. In the meantime, we are left with hope.

CHAPTER 1

"The only journey is the journey within."

—Rainer Maria Rike

What started out as an alluring wish quickly evolved into a pressing need. Things were moving too fast between us, and yet I had agreed to go on this trip with Peter. It was out of character for me to take the plunge head-on without a long, careful, and tortuous deliberation. I knew I had taken a risk, and for a risk-averse person like me, it was astonishing. But Peter had been so convincing, and deep down, I could see the logic behind his reasoning. Besides, I had other motivations.

I just had to get away...away from work, away from the people I knew and loved, away from the hustle and bustle of city life, and especially away from the long, cold winter. I needed to feel the sun on my face, the sand between my toes. I longed to hear the roar of the ocean. But above all, I needed to go to a place where no one knew me. Somewhere far away where I could unwind in peace.

I needed a break from the toxic environment that permeated the office. The Canadian brokerage firm had outsourced its operations, and we had no control over the decisions that were imposed upon us. Our foreign parent company had assured us they had the expertise to make us better. They were wrong. Our small firm had nurtured close relationships with customers and offered unique personal services. But our parent company did not configure that into their "formula." NorthWealth Investments was never the same again. Morale was low, many customers had left unsatisfied with the scaled-down service provided, and the firm was losing money every day. I wanted out, but I was hanging onto the rumour that we were up for sale and that a severance package was waiting for us. I had enjoyed my job before the changes: clients were pleasant, my coworkers were like family, and I loved my boss. But the company was broken now. Stress and anxiety had begotten all of us, and we all wore it differently. Some drank, some smoked obsessively, and some just complained—all day, every day. The strain and fear of losing our jobs had infected our environment. I had tried to put on a brave face for my team. I didn't want to contribute to the negativity. Why make it worse? But it was exhausting. I couldn't take it anymore. I needed to get away from everything and everyone.

Peter and I had researched several exotic destinations. We were overwhelmed with alluring choices. But something kept bringing us back to Roatan. Maybe it was the intimacy of the tiny island, or perhaps the idea of visiting a place unlike either of us had experienced before. It was our first trip together. We had met online a few months before, and we quickly learned that we had a lot in common. We had both recently come out of incompatible long-term relationships. We wanted to take things slow. We both wanted companionship and loved to travel. Roatan would be a test for us. It would either bring us closer or drive us apart. That's how I believed new relationships were made or broken.

I have always loved the excitement of being in an aircraft and taking off. It's the ultimate feeling of freedom, flying high above the clouds. The anticipation of the vacation was almost as much fun as the journey itself. I always insisted on reserving the window seat. I needed to visually witness myself rising above the city for my vacation to begin. It was a bonus that I wouldn't need to make small talk with a stranger beside me. Peter and I had an understanding. We were comfortable just being next to each other. We didn't feel the need to chat incessantly. I was an introvert, and Peter understood the virtue of silence.

Our vacation was officially underway. Soon after the plane gained enough altitude, I excused myself and made my way down the narrow aisle to the restroom. I couldn't help but notice a group of loud young girls already pestering the flight attendant for drinks. There were four or five of them. I could not tell exactly how many there were as they kept switching seats. One woman next to the window did not seem to be enjoying herself like the others. She did not appear to be part of the group, and looked uncomfortable. Sitting among a bunch of rambunctious young party girls, she was fidgeting, nervously looking at the back of the airplane for an empty seat. There were none. She pulled a pair of earplugs from her bag, inserted them in her ears, lowered her seat, and closed her eyes. She remained in that position for the entire duration of the flight.

On my way back from the restroom, I passed by the rowdy group and saw the poor woman, who had pulled a blanket over her for warmth.

I felt sorry for her. Perhaps she and her husband were sitting apart. It was a full flight and unless you had booked seats early, you would be out of luck.

After a short flight and a smooth landing, our plane rolled slowly along the runway until it reached its designated slot in front of a tiny terminal. There was no long queue of airplanes taxiing on the landing strip like in those massive airports in large cities. We exited the aircraft down portable stairs which led directly onto the hot tarmac. What a relief it was to feel the warm, tropical breeze envelop my body like a welcoming hug. The fact that remote Roatan had an international airport was impressive. There were only two aircraft parked on the tarmac, ours and another which had arrived earlier from Toronto. The two planes towered over the little terminal while excited passengers hurried like ants to get inside and secure their spot in the customs line.

Somehow Peter and I found ourselves at the very end of the long line of animated passengers. He was annoyed, but I refused to start our vacation on a sour note. I chose instead to observe my fellow Canadian travellers. "People watching"was a mindless way of amusing myself while passing the time, a bad habit I had picked up over the years. Peter and I would often make a silly game of it, imagining what others were thinking and saying. I tried to lighten Peter's mood by engaging him in a "round."

"Hey sweetheart, check out the single guy over there eyeing the young woman with the rose tattoo on her ankle," I murmured quietly, so no one would hear.

Peter cracked a smile, happy to join in our little game. "Yeah, I don't blame him, he has a good view from behind!"

I smacked him playfully and replied, "Perhaps you'll have more fun on this vacation being alone? That can be arranged!"

"Hey, don't you want to stay together at least until your birthday tomorrow night? How about you let me show you a good time and, if you're disappointed, then you can decide if you want to part ways," Peter joked.

"Promises, promises," I replied with a mischievous grin. "We'll see about that."

As the line moved forward around the corner, I found myself facing the young woman with the rose tattoo. She was the same woman who had that window seat, next to the rowdy girls on the plane. I'd not taken a closer look at her before. She was a strikingly beautiful woman with deep blue almond-shaped eyes framed by high cheekbones and a round face. She wore her long black hair tied in a ponytail. But when I closely observed her, I thought that she looked somewhat ill at ease. She was holding onto her purse tightly against her chest while at the same time taking furtive looks around her. My initial thought was that perhaps she was feeling insecure traveling alone.

The customs line moved quickly and, after a few routine questions, we were whisked through to a large room where we were pleasantly surprised to find our luggage waiting for us in a neat row along the wall.

"Welcome to Roatan!" shouted an airport worker in perfect English. "Please grab your bags and make your way to the exit. Look for a guide wearing an orange shirt. The guide will arrange your transfer to your resort."

We identified our guide easily and were asked to board a minibus, which already seemed full to its capacity. The tour rep insisted there were two seats left, but when Peter and I peeked inside, we saw none. The rep swiftly stepped inside and unfolded two seats from the floor in the middle of the aisles. The other passengers were as amused and surprised as we were to see two seats magically appear out of thin air. Peter took the pop-up seat behind me, and I was left with the other seat, which happened to be beside the young single woman from the plane. There was virtually no room between us, and we ended up bumping shoulders at every twist and turn on the road. After the third shoulder contact, I decided that it was time for me to introduce myself.

"Hi, I'm Misty, and behind me is my boy-friend, Peter. I'm sorry if I keep bumping into you. We're squeezed in like sardines in this bus."

She shrugged. "Don't worry about it. We'll get to the resort soon enough. At least I hope so," she said. "I'm Julia."

"Nice to meet you, Julia. Is it your first time in Roatan?"

Julia hesitated for a moment before answering my question, then smiled at me and said, "No, I've been here before, several years ago." Her smile faded quickly as she turned her head to look out the window. I was not sure what she was looking at, but I took it as my cue to end our little conversation.

Meanwhile, the booming voice of our tour guide at the front of the minibus was calling for our attention.

"Welcome to Roatan! Your vacation starts now my friends! We are so happy you chose our beautiful island for your holiday destination. It's about a forty-minute ride to the resort, so sit back, relax, and enjoy the scenery!"

As our little tour bus travelled along the only through road on the island, the young guide took the opportunity once again to proudly introduce his homeland.

"Folks, may I have your attention? Allow me to fill you in about our beautiful island. Roatan was a British colony before it was returned to Honduras, its rightful owner. That's why English is the first language, and Spanish is the second. That's not the case for the mainland, Honduras, where only Spanish is spoken. Roatan has a population of about ninety-five thousand, and our main industries are tourism and real estate development. Roatan is a small island. It's only forty miles long and barely three miles wide. Despite its small size, Roatan has become a popular destination for scuba divers from all over the world as the island is situated alongside the world's second-largest barrier reef. Fortunately for business on the island, Roatan has recently become a popular cruise ship port, with over a million cruisers per year visiting for short day trips."

I was listening intently to what the tour guide was telling us when suddenly Julia's cell phone rang. She quickly shut it off and placed it on the corner of her seat.

Peter tapped me on the shoulder to point out a view of a massive cruise ship docked at a marina. The ship appeared oddly out of proportion, towering over the little town. Out of the corner of my eye, I spotted the handsome guy who had checked out Julia earlier. He was seated at the back of the van, chatting with a young couple. I took a better look at him out of curiosity. He looked like a tall Viking with a mop of long, curly red hair. It was obvious that he'd spent a lot of time in the gym. He seemed friendly enough, chatting away with the young couple who were probably on their honeymoon, judging by the way they kept giving each other quick loving glances while holding tightly onto each other.

After another twenty minutes or so, we reached our destination, and the driver parked the bus in front of the lobby. I immediately took a liking to the resort. It was quite small in comparison to some of the massive resorts I had stayed at in Mexico. *This is charming, intimate, and quaint, just what I wished for.* I smiled excitedly at Peter.

We exited the bus and made a beeline for the lobby where we were welcomed with tropical drinks and cold snacks. The Viking was the last one to make his way to the lobby area. He was holding onto Julia's distinct rose-decorated cell phone, but he did not seem to know to whom it belonged. I approached him and pointed to Julia, who was busy checking in at the front desk. "I think you have that young lady's phone."

His face lit up, and he quickly took off without thanking me.

"Excuse me, miss, is this your phone?" he asked Julia while dawning a handsome smile.

"Oh...um, yes, thanks," she said softly, without making eye contact. She grabbed the phone and quickly turned her attention back to the check-in attendant.

As the guy with the mop of red hair returned to the back of the line, Peter nudged him as he passed us and said, "Hey, buddy, that didn't go exactly as you'd hoped, eh?"

"Yeah, strike one, and I haven't even checked in yet."

"Don't worry, there are plenty of good-looking fish in the ocean, and we are literally steps away!"

I rolled my eyes, not believing my ears. I was disappointed with Peter's rather immature behavior. I had little patience for childish jokes.

"I'm Misty, and this is Peter." I introduced ourselves still fuming at the brief exchange between Peter and the fellow with red hair.

"Pleased to meet you both, I'm Scott."

"Have you been to Roatan before, Scott?" I asked.

"No, It's my first time. I'm a scuba diver, and I've always wanted to go diving here. It's supposed to be one of the best places for deep-sea dives in the world. Do you guys scuba dive?"

"No, but we do enjoy snorkeling," I said.

"There should also be some great spots here for that."

We had just reached the front of the line, and it was our turn to check in. Peter turned around to tease Scott one more time.

"Scott, maybe we'll see you later. I could give you some good pick up lines over drinks."

This time I was truly annoyed with Peter. Had I misread him? Our relationship was relatively new, and I realized that I had much to learn about Peter. *Hopefully I'd not be disappointed. It would be a shame. Peter has so much potential.*

"I am sure Scott can hold his own, Peter. I don't think he needs any help!" My tone was sharp, and Peter picked it up right away. He gave Scott a quick glance, more like a silent warning. Scott nodded, ducking his head a bit, so as not to be too obvious.

"Miss!" We heard someone shouting loudly, and the three of us looked back at the same time to see what was going on at the front desk.

"Miss, miss, your cell phone." The concierge was calling out to Julia.

"She forgot her phone, again? My God, where is her head?" Scott said, grinning mischievously.

"Come on guys, maybe she just wants to unplug," I quipped.

Peter shook his head at Scott, wanting to defuse what might turn out to be a potentially explosive situation. "Oh babe, you're so right. Scott, give the girl some slack. She's on vacation like all of us. It's time to relax, we don't need our damn phones!"

Peter had said the right thing this time. But did he really mean it, or was he simply trying to patronize me? I took a long hard look at him. He was smiling at me.

Who's the real Peter?

CHAPTER 2

"Magic is believing in yourself."

—Unknown

The check-in was a breeze. A short lineup, a friendly receptionist, the room ready—what more could a girl ask for? It was therefore not a difficult decision to take the scenic route on our way to our room. The grounds were beautifully manicured with winding paths and tropical landscaping. The resort had an infinity pool which was the focal point of the property, hence the name of this exquisite hideaway, Infinity Bay. I gasped when we reached our room and realized how close we were to the ocean. We were literally just a few steps away from the beach. I had never stayed in a resort where you could smell the ocean and hear the roar of the waves from the terrace of the room.

After unpacking and refreshing ourselves, we headed for the beach bar. This time we sprinted along the corridors, pushed through the doors, reached the stairway at the back entrance, and stopped at the top of the stairs in awe.

In front of us was a beach of pure white sand and rolling sandbars. Beyond, the turquoise ocean glistened under the golden sun, which was setting in a ball of fire on the horizon. Roatan was a dream come true.

There were only a handful of guests enjoying the last rays of sunshine on lounge chairs lined up in neat rows on the beach facing the crystal blue water. The beach bar was beginning to fill up with guests ready for predinner drinks. Peter and I sat down at the last table available facing the ocean. We saw Scott at the bar ordering a drink, and Peter motioned for him to join us.

"Hey, fellow Canadians! How wonderful is this paradise, eh? Aren't we lucky to be here? Where are your drinks?"

"We just sat down, buddy. We were just taking a moment to enjoy the view," said Peter.

"Let me grab you some drinks. Margaritas, okay? Service looks better at the bar," he said as he winked at Peter and strutted to the bar counter, a few steps away from our table. It was obvious he wanted an excuse to order drinks from one of the scantily-attired barmaids.

"Hola, señoritas!" Scott said in his most flirtatious voice, so loud that we could hear him from our table.

A chubby middle-aged bartender turned towards Scott. "Sorry, the señoritas are busy, amigo. What can I get you?"

"Two margaritas for my friends over there, please."

Moments later, Scott came back to our table with the drinks. He seemed pleased with himself. I couldn't understand why. I'd seen how quickly the barman had jumped in as soon as he saw Scott ogling the barmaid.

"Gracias, amigo," Peter said with a wide grin.

"If you need drinks, I'm your man!" Scott replied with a knowing smile directed at Peter.

Scott's eyes suddenly lit up. "Hey guys, isn't that the girl from the reception who kept losing her cell phone?" He pointed to Julia, who was sitting at a table by herself.

I turned my head and immediately recognized her. "Yes, that's Julia. I met her on the bus."

"Do you guys mind if I go over there and invite her to join us?"

"Go ahead, Scott, but please try not to be too pushy. Don't pressure her. She may want to be left alone."

Julia appeared deep in thought when Scott approached her. She was only a few meters away, and I couldn't help myself from trying to listen to their conversation.

"Excuse me, miss."

Seeming a bit startled, Julia looked up at Scott. "Do I know you?"

"Not really, but I recognize you from the bus. I was the one who found your phone and returned it back to you when you were checking in."

"Oh, um, yes, thanks again for that," said Julia with a half-smile.

Scott flashed a broad grin. "Would you like to join me and that couple over there for cocktails?" Scott said, his finger pointed in our direction.

"Oh…um…thanks, but I don't think I'm up for socializing tonight. I'm a bit tired and don't think I'd be very good company. Thanks for the invitation, though. Some other time perhaps."

"Hey, no worries, miss. If you change your mind, feel free to join us later. It's a small resort, so I'm sure we'll see you around. My name is Scott by the way, and my Canadian friends over there are Misty and Peter."

"Thanks, Scott." She stared at him for a moment, appraising him, making up her mind whether to introduce herself, and finally gave in. "Nice to meet you, Scott. My name is Julia."

"Cool, some other time. Enjoy this wonderful evening," Scott said smiling and walked back to our table.

"What happened over there, buddy?" Peter asked teasingly.

"She wants to be alone, and I have to respect that. You know, she seems a bit out of it. Maybe it's the flight? But she didn't look very happy for someone on vacation."

"She seems nice enough, but maybe she's just shy," I put in. "I'm sure we'll see her later. In the meantime, let her have her own space...By the way, I don't know about you, but I'm starving. Let's finish our drinks and then head to dinner."

After an incredible buffet, Peter wanted to go for a walk to check out the à la carte restaurant for my birthday on the following day.

"If the place is not to your liking, we can venture off the resort," Peter suggested.

Scott decided to accompany us in our search for a suitable place to have dinner. Peter had taken a liking to Scott, and after our conversation earlier at the bar, I also warmed up to him somewhat. Behind his bravado, which I discovered at a later point was more of a façade, I realized that he could be in fact charming and even sensitive. Unfortunately, the good vibes I felt for him did not last long. As soon as he noticed the pretty barmaid cleaning the tables by the pool, Scott couldn't help himself and eagerly approached her.

Scott ran his fingers through his hair and gave the barmaid a wide smile. "Excuse me, señorita. Can you please tell me where we can find the resort's à la carte restaurant?"

The barmaid stopped what she was doing and gave Scott a quick glance over. Satisfied, she awarded Scott with her well-practiced business smile and pointed in the direction of the beach bar.

Following her instructions, we passed by the pool area and arrived at what looked like a beachside cafe, still uncertain as to where we would find the restaurant. I noticed how intimate the area had become. There were now lanterns on the tables and the waitstaff were dressed in more formal attire. *What a transformation from a few hours earlier.* In a corner, next to the bar, was an acoustic guitarist singing one of my favourite bossa nova songs, "The Girl from Ipanema."

Scott led us to the bar and asked the jolly bartender about the location of the restaurant.

"Amigo, you are in it. This beach bar becomes the most romantic place on the entire island every evening. Many customers have written to us over the years, telling tales of how they fell in love in this restaurant, on this sand where you are now standing in amazing Roatan."

Peter turned towards me, "Hon, is this where you would like to have your birthday dinner tomorrow night?"

"Yes, I would love to, Peter!"

The bartender was observing us all this time. He sure knew how to throw a hooking line, and he kept smiling at us, waiting to see the effect of his salesmanship. But in this case, he did not have to—I was sold.

"We would like to reserve a table for two for dinner tomorrow evening." Peter said.

The bartender clasped his hands as if he was about to pray. And with a sad face, he said, "I'm so sorry folks, we are all booked for tomorrow night."

"But it's my sweetheart's birthday, and we want to go somewhere special. Can you please squeeze us in?" Peter pleaded.

"I understand you want to treat your beautiful lady," the barman said, smiling at me. "You are in Roatan, and in Roatan, we like to please our guests. So, my friend, don't you worry. We will take good care of you. There are a number of great restaurants along the beach. My favourite is Vintage Pearl. I'm sure your sweet lady will love it. It's intimate, very romantic, and has a great selection of vintage wines. I strongly recommend it. If you want to check it out, go for a stroll along the beach that way. It's less than a ten-minute walk."

Meanwhile, Scott had taken a seat at the bar. Perhaps the pretty barmaids had something to do with it, but in any event, he did not look like he was about to go anywhere.

"Guys, go ahead if you want to check out the place. I just want to chill out here for a bit," said Scott.

Peter nodded. "Ok, we'll see you later. Cheers, buddy."

Peter held my hand as we walked along the beach shore. Perched high above the ocean, the moon was a bright yellow, and its reflection on the water undulated with the waves. Other couples were strolling, and a few tourists were enjoying the moment simply lounging on the beach while sipping their drinks. *This is just perfect for our first vacation together. Romantic, picturesque, and peaceful...*

"WATER TAXI! ONLY THREE DOL-LARS TO WEST BAY!" yelled a man standing on the deck of a small motorboat.

So much for my moment of peace.

The sand was still warm on our feet as we walked hand in hand along the shoreline. A few minutes later, we saw an arrow sign pointing in the direction of Vintage Pearl. The restaurant was at the top of a small hill at the end of a narrow circuitous path. A weathered wooden door bearing a large welcome sign served as its main entrance.

"Let's go in and check out the menu," I said, pulling Peter to follow me.

I was looking forward to being spoiled on my birthday and hoped this was the place. It felt like an eternity since anyone had pampered me. God knew how much I needed it. Peter was standing beside me holding so tightly onto my hand that it almost hurt. He was a lanky looking man with a kind face and puppy dog eyes, which were what attracted me to him in the first place. He could be brusque and impatient at times, but I attributed that to the fact that he was an only child and was accustomed to getting his way for most of his life. Like me, he had faced many challenges with past relationships. Many had failed because of his need for perfection.

I had met Peter online. It was not my ideal way to meet someone with whom I'd possibly spend my life. But after a long dry spell, I'd finally given in to my best friend's suggestion. "What do you have to lose," she kept telling me. After several long exchanges of text messages, some very short at the beginning and then progressively longer as we felt we were getting to know each other better, I finally decided to take the plunge, not without much trepidation. I had agreed to meet Peter in a coffee shop, the best neutral and safe spot I could think of.

When I walked in Peter was already seated, consuming a coffee while facing the entrance. He looked as nervous as I was. He was handsome, not in a classical way, more like that famous actor in those action movies. I immediately liked what I saw but remained very cautious. I had been fooled by appearances before.

Our conversation for the first ten minutes or so was stilted. There were long silent pauses as we were struggling to find something in common to talk about. Something neutral to be sure. Nonconfrontational if at all possible. And yes, most definitely a topic demonstrably engaging and interesting for both of us, or so we thought. When we broached the subject of relationships, he told me that he was looking for a good friend, someone he could talk to without fear of judgement. I smiled at his response, and we clicked immediately. At that moment we finally felt comfortable enough to speak our minds. It opened a floodgate. We could not stop talking about our past lives, our aspirations, our unsuccessful attempts at meaningful relationships, and how we found it so difficult to truly connect with anyone. We ended up laughing like two teenagers when we realized that although we came from different backgrounds, we in fact shared similar interests. We thought that we understood each other. I guess that's what brought us together. So at the end of our first date, we agreed to see each other again. And after several satisfying dates, here we were now, in Roatan, looking to take our relationship to the next level.

It took many twists and turns to get us to where we ended up. Like most new relationships, our courtship was exciting and full of hope—long walks along the shoreline of Lake Ontario while holding hands, movies, pub nights, and many tight hugs and passionate kisses. And we talked like long lost friends at their first reunion. We talked relentlessly about everything and nothing. We talked about our past relationships, reminisced about our childhood experiences, and laughed at our teenage years' misadventures. We shared memories of our college years and made fun of our likes and dislikes. We hesitantly probed about our dreams and expectations, hoping that they will be compatible. At times it felt as if we were running a marathon, rushing to learn as much as possible about each other. We felt at ease in each other's company and often wondered what would have been if we had not agreed to go along with our first blind date.

There was one topic that we did not broach in any length. I was ready to talk about our parents, but Peter quickly changed the subject. I must have touched a sensitive nerve, and I decided to let it go for the time being. The same thing happened when I asked him if he had any siblings. Something about this subject made him feel sad, and I later learned that he was an only child. He told me that he always felt like he had missed something in his life. As a young boy, he prayed for a little brother or sister. That was not to be the case. The divorce of his parents put an end to his dream, and he confessed to me that he grew up a lonely child.

After a particularly wonderful meal at a restaurant on Marine Parade Drive, Peter told me that he wanted more out of our relationship. He felt ready for a more serious commitment. I was not so sure. There was something important about me I had not found the courage to tell him. It was not physical, but I was fearful that it would appear like a scar on my face. My reticence to reveal my little secret was not borne out of shame, but it made me guarded. Perhaps I feared that he would not understand, or maybe I was simply afraid to reveal to him that I was not the perfect woman he made me out to be. But he kept insisting throughout the dinner that it was time for us to take the plunge. Once he had made up his mind, he would not give up, no matter the amount of resistance.

Peter's wish for a deeper relationship did not come to me as a total surprise. He kind of hinted at it many times over the course of our dates. I just did not think it would come to a head so soon. There was no room for escaping it any longer, it was time for me to make a decision. I could not hold him back anymore for fear that he might think that I did not share his feelings. When I stared at his pleading eyes, I knew at that moment that I had to make up my mind or stood the chance of losing him. Sensing my indecision, Peter came to the rescue with a suggestion.

"How about we get out of this town together? We could go on a trip to some exotic place. What better way to get to know each other even more and celebrate our relationship!"

I mulled over his proposal for a while, poking at the food on my plate with my fork. In the end, I did what I had done so many times in the past.

"It's a wonderful idea, Peter. Let me think about it," I said while staring at his eyes, which carried more than a trace of disappointment.

I studied him carefully for a while longer, then hedged. "Don't misunderstand me, it's a fantastic thought, but I need to sort out a few things at work first. You know, existing work commitments, availability of time off, finding someone to cover for me, these sorts of things."

Peter had lost his happy face. But he recovered quickly, not one to give up easily.

"Do that. In the meantime, I'll research some promising destinations I've in mind."

We finished our dinner and left the restaurant unsure of ourselves. We had reached an inflection point in our relationship. We both knew it, and we were both aware that nothing would be the same between us from that point on. I kept quiet on the way back to my home, walking at a steady pace while controlling my breathing. We kissed good night at my doorstep, and I rushed inside my condo, heading straight for the bathroom. Once I recovered, I decided that I had to be totally honest with Peter. *No holding back this time.* And then hopefully, our first trip together would work out just fine.

We walked into the restaurant still holding hands. It was just like the barman had told us—a warm, quaint, and welcoming little place. The hostess smiled at us as we approached her. There were no more than a half a dozen tables. Across from the bar, a waitress was busy folding red napkins. The décor was far from sophisticated but the aroma escaping from the kitchen told another story. I definitely liked this restaurant and prayed there would be a table available for us.

"Oh Peter, this is perfect," I gushed.

Peter looked happy when the hostess nodded at his request to make reservations for tomorrow night. I squeezed his hand before stepping outside to allow him to make the arrangements. A young couple smiled as they passed by and waved at me. *Who wouldn't be happy in this paradise?* As I watched the moon's light dance on the ocean, I felt a sense of utter peace overwhelm me. "Thank you, Roatan," I whispered to myself.

"Hey, sweetheart, I made a reservation for tomorrow night at 8:00 o'clock. Is that alright?"

"It's more than alright. I am so happy to be sharing my birthday with you."

Peter pulled me towards him and kissed me hard. He looked into my eyes and whispered in my ear, "I love the new Misty. You seem so relaxed. I'm so relieved to see you like this."

I smiled, feeling happy. "It's good to be away from the office, Peter. I guess I didn't realize how much my job had been draining me. I've been unhappy working in that place for far too long. And for what? For the hope of a severance package that may never come. You know what? At this moment, here on this wonderful island, with you...I realize there is more to life than staying in a dead-end job for fear of what I may lose. In the meantime, I'm losing precious years of my life. Can you believe I had to travel all this way to figure this out?"

"You needed to step away from it to see it clearly. Maybe you should submit your resignation when we get back to Toronto?"

"Yes, I think it's time," I said without hesitation. I realized this was the first meaningful decision I'd made for my own good in a very long time. "Darling, let's lighten up and enjoy the moment. Let's go back to the beach bar. I could really use a drink." I grabbed Peter's arm and led us in the direction of our resort. I was happy, and I wanted the whole world to know it.

"That's my girl!"

As we approached the beachside bar, we saw a couple on the beach. The man was sitting on the sand beside a woman on a reclining chair. The man had his back to us, and the woman was covering her face with her hands. It looked like she was crying.

"Uh oh, look at those two, hon. Looks like trouble in paradise," Peter said with a frown.

"I bet you it's his fault."

Peter gave me a puzzled look. "Why do you assume the man is at fault?"

"It usually is!" I blurted out and immediately regretted it.

What is the matter with me? I need to get over the blame game if I want to make things work with Peter.

"Sorry hon, I should never have assumed that without a good reason."

Peter smacked my butt, playfully scolding me. I glanced over at the woman sobbing.

"Peter, it's Julia!"

"Is that Scott with her?"

"What do you think is going on?"

"My god, you're right hon. That's strange… They just met. Should we go talk to them?"

"No, no, we shouldn't interfere. Let's give them some time to settle whatever is going on between them. Come, let's go. We can always sit at the bar and keep an eye on them from there."

We chose a spot facing the beach, and as soon as we were seated, the bartender chirped, "Amigos! What can I get you?"

"Dos pinot grigios, por favor." Peter was always trying to impress me with his knowledge of Spanish, even though his vocabulary was limited to a few words, usually about drinks and greetings…and a few swear words.

I gave Peter's arm a tug, "Can you see Julia and Scott from here Peter? I can't see them… The palm tree is in my way."

"Yes, I can see them now. They're talking, and it doesn't look like she's crying anymore. Let's enjoy our drinks. I'm sure they will be fine."

Before I had a chance to reply, Peter turned to look at the large TV screen above the bar. "Oh look, the Toronto Maple Leafs playoff game is on!"

"Here you go!" The bartender handed us our wine. "We show all the Leaf games at the bar since so many of our guests are from Canada.

And by the way, drinks are free during hockey night in Roatan! Go, Leafs, Go!"

"How nice of you. Free drinks in an all-inclusive resort! You gotta love this bartender. And what a treat it is to be watching hockey on the beach with my best girl! Life is good! Cheers, hon!"

"Cheers, sweetheart!" I had to shout in order to hear myself. I leaned over to give Peter a peck on the cheek. Out of the corner of my eye, I was able to see beyond the palm tree where Scott and Julia had been sitting.

They were gone.

CHAPTER 3

The best and the worst thoughts may reside in your mind at the same time. It's up to you to decide which one to listen to.

I woke up the next morning to Peter's attempt at singing to me in bed. "Happy birthday to you! Happy birthday to you!"

I slowly opened my eyes not knowing where I was. Peter's voice was the only familiar sound. I looked around, and it finally dawned on me. I was no longer in my bed in Toronto.

The room was spacious and aside from the oversized king bed, few other furnishings filled the empty space. Two small side tables, a bamboo couch facing an armchair, and a couple of suitcases placed neatly against the far wall gave the room a zen-like touch.

The single window seemed disproportionally small and left the room in a constant state of semidarkness for most of the day. The room was partially lit that morning by a single ray of sunlight that had managed to sneak in between slightly closed curtains. But somehow the room had a comfortable feel to it. Its emptiness, its lack of clutter, and its light challenge had a calming effect on me. I was awake now, fully aware of my surroundings and well rested.

"Okay, I'm awake! You're a little out of tune, but thank you for the serenade, sweetheart."

"Prepare to be spoiled today! I've got a busy day planned out for you!"

"Really? Not too busy I hope." I stretched out in bed and wondered what surprises were waiting for me.

"First breakfast at the dining room terrace followed later on with drinks by the pool. Then we hit the beach and chill until noon. After that, we can do lunch, *siesta* and chill some more.

Then the real fun starts. Dinner at Vintage Pearl at eight and then…you'll see."

"That's a full day of fun! I can't wait to see what else you've planned for me. You got me wondering, Peter!" I gave him a bright smile.

"Oh yeah, just make sure you are well rested for tonight," Peter said as he headed for the bathroom with a cheeky smirk.

Peter had the look of a satisfied man, his face glowing with energy in the early morning hours. We had made love in the middle of the night. I hadn't really been in the mood, the incident with Julia's phone was still nagging me. And I was trying to make up my mind about Peter. Was he the one? Was I the only one having doubts? This vacation together was a compatibility experiment. Better to start on a positive note. Was that not the right thing to do? At least I thought so under the circumstances. In time all will be clear. So, I responded to Peter's love making. It was less than satisfying, but better than a sleeping pill, and I fell asleep almost immediately.

After my morning shower, I was ready to celebrate my birthday all day long. It was a short walk to the dining room terrace. Along the way we took our time to enjoy the resort grounds surrounded by tall hibiscus flowers full of bright red blooms. A tiny iguana near my feet startled me, and Peter laughed at my reaction. Just ahead, a hermit crab was slowly crossing our path. As we stepped closer, the crab retreated into its shell. Below the ramp to the dining terrace was a family of cats keeping cool in the shade. They were well looked after with healthy bellies and a water dish nearby. I could have spent the whole morning in the gardens, but Peter had another idea. He gently held my arm and led me up some stairs to the terrace where a magnificent breakfast buffet was waiting for us. A friendly hostess greeted us at the door, gave a knowing smile to Peter, and led us to a table overlooking the grounds and facing the ocean.

"Look, Peter!" I said as I pointed to a large cruise ship passing by in the distance.

"It must be *The Love Boat*!" Peter laughed.

"You are so much more romantic here than back home," I said a tad mockingly.

The waitress smiled at us while pouring lemon water. "Roatan is a romantic place, miss. I met my husband here while I was working in this restaurant."

"There you go. I told you that we picked a romantic place to have our vacation."

We ordered coffee and made our way to the breakfast buffet. Peter went for the fresh fruit salad while I headed straight to the omelette station. Scott was standing in line ahead of me, wearing a brightly colored Hawaiian shirt with matching shorts and flip-flops. I stifled a giggle while thinking to myself that Scott had wasted no time going native.

"Hey, stranger!" I called out from the back of the line.

He turned around and chirped, "Good morning, beautiful! You're looking ravishing this morning."

Scott's compliment took me by surprise. Blushing, I quickly replied, "Would you like to join us for breakfast?"

"Sure, I would like that."

He waited for me while I was filling my plate, and together we walked over to join Peter.

"Well, well, well. What do I see here? I leave you alone for one minute, and you pick up another guy?" Peter teased. "What about you Scott, how are you doing this morning?"

"Great, thanks, I hope you don't mind me crashing your tête-à-tête."

"Not at all, bud. So, what do you have planned for today?"

"Going scuba diving this morning in the West End. This island is a diver's dream. At least that is what I was told by the travel agent." Scott paused for effect and grinned at Peter like he had something really special to tell us. "And later…I have a dinner date with a very beautiful woman."

"Wow, this guy moves fast! It's only our first full day here, and he's got another catch. Who is the lucky girl this time?"

"Julia. Yes, you heard me right. Julia and I are having dinner together." Scott was beaming from ear to ear.

Peter and I exchanged quick glances. I was surprised that Julia had accepted Scott's dinner invitation. What I witnessed on the beach the night before did not look promising.

The whole incident flashed back in my mind. "Scott, last night, after we went for a walk, we saw you and Julia on the beach. She was crying. What happened?" I had to ask or the matter would bother me for the rest of my stay in Roatan. I could not wait to hear Scott's explanation, even if I did not expect to hear the full truth.

"Oh, you saw us?" Scott looked uncomfortable and took a long time before answering me. "Yes... um, how should I say it? She was upset about something, but I would rather not elaborate."

I knew it! Scott was cagey, just as I suspected he would be.

"But, is she alright?" I asked.

"Oh, yes of course, she just had...what can I say...a moment. That's all. She's fine, really, nothing to worry about, Misty."

There was an awkward silence. Scott looked unsettled to me. Meanwhile Peter kept eating his breakfast, seemingly oblivious to what was being said. He shoved a large piece of pineapple in his mouth and cracked a joke, "Buddy, I hope your dinner date goes well, but be careful. The young lady looks like she's playing hard to get."

"More like a tease, if you get my gist," replied Scott.

"Guys!" I shouted, perhaps a bit too loud, as a few guests sitting nearby stared in our direction.

"What's wrong, Misty? We're just kidding around."

I swallowed hard, trying to control my temper. The last thing I wanted to do was to spoil my special day. I let the moment pass and continued eating my breakfast in silence. When we finally decided to leave, Peter and I went our own way leaving Scott behind.

After breakfast, Peter and I went back to our room to change into our bathing suits. We then made our way to the beach, where we found two lounge chairs under a palm tree with a stunning view of the ocean. The sky was clear, and the water was calm. I stretched my body on the chair, took a deep breath, and before long fell into a deep sleep.

Perhaps it was the hot Caribbean sun, the salt in the air, or the rhythmic snoring of Peter lying beside me that awakened me suddenly in the middle of my nap. But there was something else. When I looked over at Peter, he was deep asleep. It took me a while to figure out that the ping of my iPhone was the culprit. I heard it again and debated whether I should check if I had any messages. In the end my curiosity got the better of me, and I reached for my phone. I had seven new text messages. They were all texts from family and friends wishing me a happy birthday. I was thrilled that so many people cared about me. *How lucky am I to have such wonderful people in my life.* And then a strange thought came to me, something so weird that it frightened me. *If I died today, I would die truly happy.* How many people would think that on the day of their birthday? I chased away the terrible thought from my mind and turned my attention to Peter, who was still sleeping peacefully on the lounge chair beside me. I smiled at him and felt reassured.

"BANANA BREAD! BANANA BREAD! COCONUT CANDY!" shouted one of the beach vendors who frequently roamed the resort. He was loud but not overly aggressive like the other vendors, and I admired his enthusiasm. He stopped to chat with another vendor passing by. He was an old man wearing a large hat made of braided palm leaves, who was selling handmade toy helicopters. The old man was not much of a talker from what I could observe from his brief interaction with the other vendor. He quickly picked up the goods that he had placed on a worn mat on the sand and hobbled off looking for another spot along the beach. He hopped along in the deep sand on one leg while leaning on a crutch to help him walk.

I watched him until he finally settled down on a spot surrounded by several potential customers. That's when I noticed Julia on a lounge chair sitting alone nearby. We exchanged a quick glance, and I decided to walk over to her.

"Good morning, Julia."

"Good morning, Misty."

Her tone was not too inviting, and my attempt at a light conversation about the beauty of the resort grounds and beach did not go well. She was polite but somewhat distant, sticking to one-word answers to most of my questions. I was not getting anywhere and after a few attempts at breaking the ice, I finally decided to tell her what was on my mind.

"We bumped into Scott at breakfast this morning. He mentioned you two are having dinner tonight."

Julia pushed her hair behind her ears in one swift motion. "Oh yes...we are supposed to but... I don't know if I should. Maybe I'll cancel," she looked away seemingly deep in thought.

"Oh? Why not, is everything okay?"

"Yes, um, I'm just tired, and I don't think I'll be good company." She shrugged and looked away again.

It was clear there was something bothering Julia, and she was not about to give me her reasons. I did not think that she mistrusted me. I simply thought that maybe she just wanted to be left alone. But what really annoyed me was that I could not get a good read on her. She seemed blasé and somewhat aloof. I could not figure out if she liked Scott or not. She certainly was interested enough to have accepted to have dinner with him, although she was clearly hedging now. But then why the sudden cold shoulder? I wished her a good day and excused myself, feeling somewhat baffled by her behavior. *What is she not telling me? What did Scott say, or do to make her cry?*

Peter was awake when I returned to our spot under the palm tree. I didn't feel the need to tell him about my brief encounter with Julia. Not yet, at least. Nor did I share my concerns about Scott. Above all, I needed time to process my interaction with Julia.

Peter and I spent a leisurely morning and afternoon on the beach until sunset. Early evening was my favourite time to be by the ocean. The crowd was gone, and a cool breeze filled the air. The sun was slipping below the horizon. Soon it would disappear leaving a few sun worshippers lazing on the beach. When it became too dark, Peter and I went for a long stroll along the shore. I loved walking barefoot in the sand at the edge of the water. I adored the feeling of my feet sinking into the wet sand. I liked seeing the imprints my feet left behind and enjoyed watching wave after wave erase any trace of my tracks, like the passage of time.

Soon it was time to freshen up for our dinner at Vintage Pearl. We walked past the beach bar on the way to our room. It was crowded with tourists enjoying happy hour.

"Hey, hon, let's stop in for a cocktail after we change for dinner," Peter said enthusiastically.

"Twist my rubber arm," I happily retorted.

By the time we made it to the bar, it was already crowded with hockey fans. It was a lively group and judging by the quantity of beer flowing, I guessed most of them were Canadian tourists. Luckily for us, we found the last two spots at the very end of the bar. Peter struck up a conversation with a fellow Torontonian beside him. Although it was only 7:30 p.m., we were able to catch the Leafs game thanks to the two-hour time difference. Toronto was tied with Washington in the second period. I normally wouldn't care, but it was the first time the Leafs had made the playoffs in years. Toronto fans were loyal and still held out hope for the Stanley Cup they have not won since 1967. We watched the game like true hockey fans, screaming when one of the Leafs players was hooked illegally (in our opinion), gave high fives when the Leafs scored, and managed to gulp large amounts of beer at every opportunity. During a commercial break I struggled to pull Peter away from the game. On my third attempt, I succeeded in getting his full attention by reminding him that we had reservations at Vintage Pearl.

We walked hand in hand to the restaurant. The hostess recognized us immediately and greeted us with a warm smile. She led us to the bar where we enjoyed a glass of white wine while waiting for our table to be set. Our table was situated in a private alcove in the corner of the room, and someone had placed a small bouquet of red roses in the middle. We were seated close to an acoustic guitar player, who was singing a tune she had composed about Roatan. As she sang, I felt shivers all over my body, moved by her passionate rendition of her beautiful lyrics.

The waitress handed us the menu, and I felt like a kid in a candy store when I saw the wine list. Peter knew I loved my wine, and he wanted to indulge me.

"Treat yourself to the very best, honey, it's your birthday."

The restaurant was nearly full to capacity with mostly locals, which I took as a good sign. At the suggestion of our waitress, we picked a delicious coconut stew for our main course. We later learned that it was one of Roatan's most famous specialties.

"I've never seen you so radiant," said Peter. I felt his hand caressing my thigh to the beat of the music. His eyes were watching my every move while I was sipping my wine. His hand inched forward under my dress, and he squeezed me gently. I felt my heart quiver. I put down my wine glass on the immaculate white tablecloth, and he leaned forward and reached for my lips. He tasted of wine and rosemary. He held my hand and kissed each one of my fingers one at a time while staring into my eyes. I knew at that moment he was madly in love with me.

"It has been a long time since I felt this happy. This is the best birthday present. Thank you so much, sweetheart."

He leaned over and gave me another deep kiss. He then excused himself, and I saw him chat briefly with the waitress. Moments later, she came out with a large piece of cheesecake topped with Irish cream—my favorite dessert—and a candle in the middle. As she placed the cake on the table in front of me, the guitarist began playing a classic rendition of "Happy Birthday." I was completely overwhelmed with emotion, and I began to cry.

"Thank you," I managed to mumble softly between tears. The waitress smiled and asked if I wanted another glass of wine. I hesitated for an instant. I was already feeling a bit light-headed, but I didn't want the evening to end.

"Yes, please bring another bottle," Peter answered for me.

We enjoyed our wine while being serenaded by the guitarist. A lovely evening went by, so enchanting that I didn't realize that we were the only guests left in the restaurant.

"This was wonderful Peter, thank you for the best birthday ever."

"It's not over yet honey. It's only eleven o'clock. Let's go back to our room and have a nightcap on the terrace."

"Ok, but I'll need you to help me get there. I think I've had a bit too much wine."

"Don't worry, I'll take care of you."

I'll take care of you, I mouthed Peter's words to myself. I loved hearing those words. They comforted me and made me feel safe. *When was the last time someone really took care of me? My parents, when I was a child, perhaps?* For sure, many friendships had blossomed over the years with some of my colleagues at work. But it only meant a few drinks after work at the nearby pub. Nothing more. I dreaded weekends, but strangely enough, I looked forward to Monday mornings. Work filled my time and made me feel like I had a purpose. I'd had some brief relationships, some even meaningful while they lasted, but none made me feel the way I felt with Peter right now. Peter said he will take care of me. *I like so much the way it sounds.*

But still, there was something about Peter that I could not figure out. He could be kind and generous. He could be a good listener when it mattered. His attention span was amazing for issues he deemed important. But when he made up his mind about something he cared for, the force of a hurricane could not sway him. It was an admirable yet frustrating quality. I once told him that he could be stubborn. He took it well and explained to me that it was not out of stubbornness that he was set in his ways. If you care deeply about something or someone, he said to me, there's no other way—you must hold on firmly to that belief.

After dinner, we strolled along the beach. It was a full moon and a warm tropical breeze brushed my face. We soon approached the resort bar where the crowd had doubled in size, and a wild party was going on. Peter let go of my hand and walked a few steps ahead of me, his gaze fixated on the large screen above the bar. I caught up with him as he spotted the hockey fan he had been chatting with earlier.

"Hey, buddy, what happened with the game?"

"The Leafs won in overtime! A real nail-biter, man. We're celebrating. Come join us."

Peter was excited to hear the news and looked at me for approval. I looked back at him and shook my head. I couldn't believe he wanted to end the most perfect evening of my life this way.

Peter quickly realized his mistake and told the hockey fan, "Sorry bud, please have a drink for me. We have better plans for tonight."

"I don't blame you, buddy!" The hockey fan said with a smirk on his face. "Go, Leafs, Go!" He shouted while holding his beer bottle high above his head.

Peter gave him a thumbs up, and we walked back to our room arm- in-arm. I held onto him tightly.

I was on cloud nine.

CHAPTER 4

*The light will guide you if you allow
it to shine.*

I woke up the next morning not knowing where I was. The room was bright, and I could hear Peter in the shower. I sat up and immediately felt dizzy. I knew I had too much wine to drink the night before. *Did we end up having more drinks on the terrace last night?* I could not remember. In fact, everything that happened after our dinner was a total blur. I laid down again and hoped the dizziness would soon pass. Peter came out of the washroom clean-shaven and full of energy. He took one look at me and tried to snap me out of my doldrums.

"Good morning, hon! Did you sleep well?" He said with an impish grin.

"Not so well, and it's not funny. I think we drank the same amount of wine, but it looks like I'm the only one suffering the consequences! Did we drink on the terrace last night?"

"No hon, when we got back to the room you headed straight to bed and passed out in no time at all. Nothing could wake you. Believe me, I tried."

"Oh, wow. I'm such a bad date. I can't hold my liquor, my darling. So sorry about that, I'm a bit embarrassed."

Peter was amused. I could see that he was tempted to jump back in bed with me but one look outside the window changed his mind. "Sweetheart, please get up. It's a beautiful sunny day out there. Let's get out of the room and enjoy our time on the beach!"

I hushed him away and got up from the bed. After a quick shower, and after carefully applying suntan lotion all over my body, I was ready for a full day on a hot, sandy beach. I was glad that I was wearing my dark sunglasses when I stepped out. I'd not have made it past the lobby otherwise. The sun was bright, and I was still feeling woozy. I followed Peter gingerly to the beach, one slow and unsteady step at a time. I heard a ping from my phone. A WhatsApp incoming call from my bestie. I had to answer. I told Peter to keep walking while I answered the phone.

"Hey, Lucy!"

"Happy belated birthday girlfriend! How did it go last night with your Prince Charming?"

"Oh my God, it was the best night ever! Peter took me to the most charming little restaurant on the beach. We had vintage wine, delicious food and…"

"Yes, I'm sure it was all perfect, but what about *dessert*?"

"You mean get straight to the good part?"

"Uh…yeah."

"Well, after a romantic walk along the beach to our hotel, we went back to our room and…"

"And?"

"And I don't remember anything, but I woke up the next morning in bed feeling dizzy!"

"Were you naked?"

"Lucy!"

"What?"

"You're so nosy!"

"That's what you love about me! You know you can tell me anything. No judgement."

"No judgement." It was a pact we had honored since we were in our teens.

"So, hurry up and get to the good part, Misty!"

"I actually had my clothes on from the night before when I woke up."

"Oh, wow that's pretty anticlimactic, Misty, sorry to hear, but at least Peter is a gentleman, so there's that."

"Lucy, I miss you. Let's have brunch when I get back."

"Of course! By then I hope you'll have some juicy stuff to tell! Enjoy paradise with the prince!"

"Thanks, Lucy! Be good!"

I rushed to catch up with Peter, and before he asked, I told him it was Lucy on the phone.

Scott saw us coming and waved, inviting us to join him. He had found a quiet spot in a shaded quiet corner of the beach.

"Hey guys, I've got prime real estate here! Please come join me."

He helped Peter gather two long chaises and as soon as we made ourselves comfortable, Scott stared at me. It felt more like an appraisal. I stared back at him waiting for him to make the first move.

"So, how was your birthday dinner last night?" Scott asked.

"It was wonderful! One I won't ever forget, thanks to Peter."

"I'll bet," Scott smirked.

"And how was your evening, Scott?" Peter asked.

"It was interesting to say the least. I met Julia for dinner at the buffet. We sat down around seven, and we ended up closing the place." Scott sat up, waiting for us to react, and since all he received from us were blank stares, he continued in his best matter-of-fact tone. "She is a really great girl…so sweet, intelligent, and genuine. We chatted about so many things. You know, we really hit it off. I felt like I could tell her anything."

Scott paused for a moment. He looked pensive, as if he was reliving the entire dinner date in his mind. All of sudden, he blurted out, "But I still think there's something off about her."

It was a strange thing to say, even for Scott. I wondered where he was heading with that comment.

"What do you mean by that, Scott?" I asked.

"Well, at first the whole dinner went very well. She even laughed at my stupid jokes, and believe me, they're not that funny."

"Well, I don't blame her. But seriously what happened that was so out of the ordinary?"

"You're funny, Misty. Anyway, when I realized that we were the only two guests left in the dining room, I touched her hand to signal that perhaps it was time to leave. That's when things got awkward. And I mean really awkward."

Peter squinted. "How so? What did she do?"

"She tensed right up and was very quiet after that. She was really fidgety and could not wait to leave the place. I walked her back to her room, thinking that she wanted to call it a night. When we reached her door, I was about to ask her if there was something wrong. But, before I had a chance to ask, she mumbled something about a nice evening and abruptly went inside her room and shut the door behind her. Needless to say, I felt like a total idiot standing at her doorstep. I didn't know if I'd done or said something that might have offended her. But the abrupt way she ended the evening with me was…how can I describe it…weird and rude?"

Peter was quick to come to Scott's defense. "I don't think you did anything wrong, and you certainly didn't need to apologize for touching her hand."

"Scott, maybe she felt you were coming on too strong."

He raised his hand in protest. "I swear to you, Misty, I was the perfect gentleman."

"Then in that case, I think she must have some issues to sort out. Don't blame yourself. She might come around. Who knows what's bothering her?"

"You might be right, Misty. Anyway, there's still hope. Earlier on in the evening she agreed to have lunch with me today. We'll see how that goes."

I was trying to make sense of it all. There must be something else that Scott was not telling us. *First the tears on the beach and now the door slammed shut.* I once again chose not to share my concerns with Peter. Instead, I turned my attention to Scott and simply said, "It's a good sign, Scott. All may not be lost."

Peter looked restless in his chair and seemed to have lost interest in the conversation. He got up suddenly and said, "Hey, hon, let's go for a dip in the ocean."

I looked up at him, momentarily blinded by the sun above me. He was smiling at me, for what was meant to be an invitation. I was puzzled by the ease with which he was able to shift subjects, ready to move on as if nothing important had been said or done moments earlier. Yet, he seemed impatient at my hesitation. Something different was happening with him this time.

"A swim would do you lots of good, Misty," he said with the same plastered smile on his face.

I pulled my feet together under the chair, extending my hand for assistance, to which he obliged with a grin. What might be construed as weakness, on my part, was in fact my way to avoid arguments at any cost. Better be agreeable, nothing good ever came out of anger. At least this was one important lesson I'd retained from my last breakup. Besides, Peter might be right about the swim after all. There would be more time later on to hash out our issues after a breather.

"You lovebirds go enjoy yourselves! I'm going to have a little siesta," Scott said as he closed his eyes and pretended to fall asleep.

Peter and I had fun frolicking in the water for quite a while. A glass bottom boat passed by, and I convinced Peter to book the next tour. We rapidly gathered our things from the beach and told Scott we would see him later for drinks before dinner.

"Have a great lunch with Julia," I shouted at Scott as we left for the boat tour.

As we walked away, I reflected some more about Julia's odd conflicting behaviour. Alternating between engaging and secretive, confident and unassuming, she seemed a woman of inscrutable impulses. She was well aware of her natural beauty and the effect she had on people, yet she never imposed her presence and seemed rather uncomfortable when anyone stared at her. I wanted to spend more time with her to get to know her better, to learn about her, where she came from, what her interests were, what brought her to Roatan, travelling all alone. But she never gave me the chance, always finding an excuse to look away, disengaging from our conversation, seemingly disinterested. Yet, despite it all, I never felt that she was running away from me, rather she seemed distracted by something that was exercising a strong pull on her. In many ways, I felt sorry for Scott. Julia was indeed a handful. *What's troubling her? I could not help wondering.*

The glass bottom boat was stationed on a dock on the outer limit of the resort grounds. We paid our fare, and the boat left right away. There was only one other couple on board. As the boat sailed away, we were all told to go below deck. We descended a narrow staircase, below the hull of the boat under sea level. At the bottom was a large room that had a wooden floor and large glass windows stretching along the full length of the boat on both sides. In the middle of the room was a long bench where Peter and I sat. Soon after we were joined by the other couple, and we all sat waiting quietly for the boat to sail to the open sea. Peter and I were seated in the center of the bench in order to get a full panoramic view of the ocean's depth. The water was a bit murky as we left the docks. About ten minutes later, the boat slowed down and that's when we were treated to an incredible spectacle. Before our eyes flaunted an unimaginable sight of huge crabs crawling on the seafloor, schools of brightly colored fish of all sizes, massive pink and white coral reefs, and giant sea turtles dancing to the beat of the ocean. I recorded as much as I could with my iPhone, jumping over the bench from one side to the other, determined to capture the best shots. I was like a child in a toy store. I was so mesmerized by what I was seeing that I did not hear Peter calling my name. He finally nudged me to get my attention.

"Hey hon, I don't feel so well down here. I'm going up on deck to get some fresh air. Please stay here as long as you want. Don't worry about me, it's just a little nausea."

"Okay, sweetheart, I'll be up shortly. I just want to get a better shot of the sea turtles. It looks like we're already heading back to the dock. Hang in there."

At that point, I realized I was alone below deck. The other couple had also gone upstairs. It was my opportunity to be the lone observer of the ocean's secrets, and I took full advantage of it. I sat down on the bench and shut off my iPhone, seeking to be in full harmony with the silence of this marvelous underworld. Sadly, as we approached the docks, the beauty of the moment was broken by an unpleasant sight—a tin can stuck in the coral, an old tire half buried in the silt, and a rusted chain stuck in the sand. *What a shame.*

As I stood up to make my way upstairs, I spotted a woman's scarf snagged on one of the dock posts. It was floating rhythmically with the waves, and I thought it looked somewhat familiar. We were now docked, and Peter was calling me from the stairwell to come up on deck.

Peter wasted no time leaving the boat and scurried ahead of me along the dock leading to the beach. As I hurried to catch up with him, I noticed a very handsome, muscular young man sitting in a water taxi boat nearby. He caught me checking him out and smiled at me.

"Hola, señorita! Would you like a ride in my water taxi? This is *The Love Boat,* and I am the captain. Please come aboard, I was expecting you!"

I smiled back. "That's a tempting offer, but I don't want to upset my boyfriend." I pointed my finger to where Peter was standing on the beach. He had been watching me, and I rushed to catch up with him.

"I see you've made a new friend," said Peter as soon as I caught up with him. I could detect a hint of jealousy in his tone. It made me smile.

"Yes, he has quite a pickup line. He calls his water taxi *The Love Boat.* I bet he gives a lot of rides to the young ladies." I knew I was rubbing it in. I could not resist teasing Peter, who did not look too happy.

"I bet he does…but not the kind of rides you're talking about!"

"Oh my God, Peter! You're so gross!" I smacked him and then burst out laughing.

Peter was not amused. "I'm still feeling nauseous from the boat ride. I need to sit down."

"Why don't we lounge on the beach for a bit until you feel better? We can have a light lunch at the beachside cafe later on, if you want."

Peter jumped on the suggestion as if he wanted to get as far as possible away from the docks. After a short walk on the hot sand, we found the same lounge chairs we had used earlier. Scott was no longer there.

"I guess Scott left to get ready for his lunch date with Julia," I said.

Peter did not react to my comment and quickly made himself comfortable for a nap. It seemed like a good idea, so I decided to have one too.

I was deep asleep when something or someone woke me up. With my eyes half shut, blinded by the sun glaring down at me, I tried to make sense of what was happening. I was finally able to discern Scott hovering over me. He was speaking to me but, being still in a daze,

I could not make out a single word of what he was saying.

"It's okay, Scott, I'm awake now. There's no need to shout."

"Hey, guys, sorry to bother you. I didn't realize you were sound asleep."

"So, what's up?" A grouchy Peter asked. "You can't wait to tell us about your lunch with Julia?"

Scott looked miserable and did not hide his anger.

"She never showed up!"

Peter was now fully awake. He shook his head and blared, "You've got to be kidding me. She stood you up, man!"

"Maybe she forgot about the lunch date, Scott," I suggested. "Didn't you tell me that she seemed preoccupied?"

What I said seemed to calm him down. "Well maybe, but I don't know what's going on with her. I even went over to look for her in her room. But she wasn't there."

"What about calling or texting her?"

"I don't have her phone number. She didn't want to give it to me."

"Well buddy, I wouldn't worry so much about her. Play it cool, she may come around," said Peter.

"Yeah. But it sucks, and I don't like being stood up. Anyway, guys I'm sorry I've taken so much of your time. I feel like a good long swim right now."

We both watched Scott storm off as he headed for the beach bar. *So much for the swim,* I chuckled.

I turned to Peter, who was about to lie down. "That's odd. Do you think something's going on between those two?"

"I don't know, to be honest. I don't understand why he is so into her. She is so standoffish."

"Well, maybe she's just being cautious. She's forgetful though. Remember, she kept losing her phone when we first arrived in Roatan. But you know what, I think Scott is right about one thing. Something does seem off about her."

Peter kept tapping his fingers on the armrest. A sure sign that he had lost interest in the conversation. I chirped in, "Hey, I see that you are feeling better. Can we grab lunch at the beachside cafe? I'm starving."

"Yeah, I'm feeling much better, thanks, hon. Let's eat."

As we were gathering our things, I saw a burly security guard heading our way.

Is something wrong?

"Good afternoon, how're you guys doing today?" he asked in a deep voice.

"Just fine, sir." Peter answered for us.

"Where you folks from?" he inquired.

"Toronto," said Peter.

"Toronto? How 'bout that Leafs game last night? They sure know how to get the job done when it matters the most."

"Yeah, they won in overtime! That was awesome! Did you watch the game?" Peter was excited to talk about hockey with anyone who would indulge him.

"No, I was on duty, but I heard some guests talking about how great a game it was."

"Yeah, it's a big win for us," Peter said proudly.

"Sir, is everything ok?" I asked, wondering why he had stopped to talk to us. I could not help thinking about what Scott had told us earlier.

"Yes, ma'am. I'm just doing my rounds."

"Is it pretty safe in this area?"

"Yes, ma'am. But keep in mind that the beach is patrolled only until 10pm. After 10, there is no security presence. You shouldn't go anywhere alone after 10," he cautioned me.

"Ok, thank you for the heads up, sir."

"Enjoy your vacation, and welcome to Roatan."

"Thanks for stopping by," said Peter as the security guard turned to walk away.

"Go Leafs!" The guard pumped his fist in the air as he strolled away to chat with another couple nearby.

"That was so nice of him to stop and chat with us," I said, somewhat reassured.

"Don't be fooled by his friendly manners. He was checking our wristbands to make sure we're legitimate guests."

"Oh, you're so cynical. Can't people just be kind to one another without ulterior motives?"

Peter and I had a light lunch and then we spent the afternoon at the resort infinity pool. From where we sat, the pool gave the illusion that the water extended to the ocean. The sky was clear, and it was quite hot under the sun. We found lounge chairs under an umbrella, where I curled up with a cold drink and a book that I had started reading on the plane. Peter joined me after refreshing himself in the pool.

"Well, don't you look cozy?" he said. "Can I convince you to join me in the pool?"

"Later for sure...I'm too comfy right now, and I want to see what happens in this story I'm reading."

"That's the book your colleague at work gave you, right? The financial thriller, *Nomad on the Run*. I'm surprised you would want to read something in the finance genre while on vacation. I thought you wanted a break from all of that."

"I find it interesting, and the book is a refreshing escape for me. It's a thriller but hits on elements we can all relate to."

"Yeah, like what?" Peter asked.

"Like, when something seems too good to be true, it probably is…It's also about following our instincts. But what it really comes down to is trust…trusting yourself above all."

"Sounds quite heavy for a vacation read."

"Not really. I find it intriguing, and helpful in so many ways."

A commotion around the pool suddenly grabbed our attention. A crab had found its way into the water, and all the kids were screaming. It was quite a ruckus the kids were making, and the parents were not helping, yelling as loud as they could for security to come over immediately. It was an amusing scene to say the least.

In the corner of my eye, I noticed that Peter was no longer paying any attention to what was going on in the pool. He had spotted Scott walking in our direction. Something about Scott's demeanor had changed. Gone was the self-assured, almost arrogant look. Head hanging low, shoulders slumped, he approached us wearing a deep frown on his face.

"Now what's wrong, buddy? You look white as a sheet."

One glance at him sent my heart racing. "Did you find Julia?" I inquired.

"No."

I could tell Scott was still bothered by being stood up. "Perhaps something came up, and she didn't know how to reach you," I said, trying my best to be helpful.

"Yeah. This is a small resort, and I'm sure you'll bump into her soon," Peter added.

Scott ran his hands through his hair a couple of times. "You guys may be right. But I don't like the way she treated me. It's not right. Have you guys seen her around?"

"No, we haven't."

I gave Scott a curt reply. I definitely did not like his attitude. There could be thousands of good reasons why Julia had failed to show up, and all Scott could think about was his own bruised ego.

On the other hand, Peter took a more reassuring tone that really surprised me. "It's not the end of the world, buddy. You'll find out what happened when you see her. I'm sure she's got a good excuse for not showing up. In the meantime, try to have some fun and enjoy your vacation. Why don't you meet us at the beach bar around seven for predinner drinks?"

"Yeah, maybe I'll join you. I hope you're right about Julia, Peter." Scott then turned towards me and stared me down.

"Your girl is a keeper, buddy. She knows how to make a guy feel good," he said in a sarcastic tone addressing Peter while glaring at me.

I knew what Scott was doing. He was mad at Julia and was taking his frustration out on me. At that moment, I had two choices: reply in kind or be the better person and ignore him. Fortunately, I did not have to decide. Peter came immediately to my defense. He did not miss a beat and gave it back to Scott in kind.

"I agree with you, bud. I don't know how I got so lucky!" Peter turned to me and kissed me on the mouth. That sealed the argument.

Scott was sitting at the bar when we arrived later that evening. The sun had already set on the horizon, and the dining tables set on the sand in front of the bar had transitioned from casual beach dining into quaint romantic tables for two, adorned with white cloths and lanterns.

"Hey Scott, thanks for saving us seats," said Peter while giving his buddy a pat on the back. "What are you drinking tonight?"

"Whisky on the rocks."

Just then, the jolly bartender handed Scott a fresh drink.

"Amigos! Good evening! White wine for the lady and a beer for the gentleman."

"How did he know?" I asked Peter.

"He's really good at what he does!" Peter was no longer paying attention to Scott and me. He was busy observing the action behind the bar. "And by the looks of it, he clearly enjoys his job!" He added jokingly.

On cue, Scott and I turned our back to look at the barman, who was flirting with a pretty barmaid, his hands roaming over her backside. She had initiated a hug, and he embraced her back, dawning a huge grin. We all laughed, thankful for the break in the tension that had developed between Scott and me earlier. We quickly finished our drinks and then made our way to the dining room in the main building of the resort. The same hostess greeted us with her well-practiced warm smile.

"Good evening," said the hostess, while she made up her mind about where to seat us. "A table for four?"

"Just three tonight," I replied.

"Where's your lady friend this evening?" she asked Scott.

Scott shrugged. "I wish I knew. Did you by any chance see her today?"

"No, the last time I saw her was last night when I seated you both."

I didn't know what to make of Scott. On the one hand, I felt sorry for him. But then I thought that Julia must have had her reason for treating him the way she did. The bottom line was that I wasn't sure about Scott's intentions, and I was worried about Julia.

"Please let me show you to a table on the terrace," the ever-smiling hostess said while guiding us to a table overlooking the ocean.

When we reached the table, Scott pulled the chair out for me. *A peace gesture.*

"Thanks Scott, you're a gentleman."

A hostess turned to me, "Tonight is seafood night. Please try our grouper, which was caught today. We also have a variety of roasted herbed vegetables and our chef's specialty, ratatouille.

While you make up your mind about your order, can I get you a drink?"

"I'll start with a glass of chardonnay, please."

"Make that two, please," said Peter.

"I'll have a pinot noir, thanks," chipped in Scott.

"So, Scott, what brought you to Roatan of all places?" I asked, trying my best to keep my tone as friendly as possible.

"I love to scuba dive, as you know. What about you?" Scott said.

"Scubadiving is not for us. Personally, I had a bad experience with nausea and sea-sickness during an open water expedition. I haven't been since," I said.

"Oh, man, you guys don't know what you're missing. It's a whole other planet down there. And no videos or pictures can do justice to the actual experience."

"Sounds seriously amazing," Peter said.

"You want to know something I found strange about Julia? When I mentioned diving to her, she was totally uninterested. I never had that reaction before. I mean, I understand it's not everyone's thing. But in her case, her whole demeanor completely changed. One moment she was fully engaged in our conversation, the next I couldn't get another word out of her. You'd think, since we don't know much about each other, it would be a good subject to chat about, you know…to break the ice, so to speak."

I looked at Peter to see if he had any reaction to what Scott had just told us. But there was none. He just kept staring at Scott, with a stoic expression on his face. The standoff lasted too long, so I decided to pipe up with a note of encouragement. "Scott, I really hope you don't let your feelings about Julia affect your vacation."

He brushed his hair with the palm of his right hand. "I'm just annoyed about the whole thing because I thought that we really hit it off. I guess I must have had my signals crossed. I never thought she was the type to stand a guy up. To tell you the truth, I'm not just pissed. I'd like to know what gave her the right to treat me that way. To tell you the truth, I think it's her loss."

I no longer felt sorry for Scott after his last comments. The guy was arrogant for sure. His big ego was bruised, probably not accustomed to rejection. I was now more determined than ever to have a chat with Julia and get to the bottom of what was going on between these two.

Once again Peter tried to be helpful. I still did not understand his motivation, other than possibly one of those male bonding things.

"Don't be so hard on yourself. I have an idea, buddy. Why don't you leave her a message with the concierge asking her to call your cell? You can say that you're worried and just want to know if she is okay."

"It'll be a total waste of time!" Scott said and got up from his chair to leave. He walked away, mumbling something under his breath.

CHAPTER 5

*"I know but one freedom and that is
the freedom of the mind."*

—Antoine de Saint-Exupéry

The next day, Peter and I slept in and went for a late breakfast. It was 10:30 a.m. when we finished our morning coffee and decided it was time for another blissful day on the beach. The weather forecast app on my phone said it was 25°C and clear skies the entire day.

We parked ourselves under an umbrella, as close as possible to the water. I felt the most at peace with myself in as long as I could remember. I had no interest in reading the news or checking in with the office. I simply wanted to enjoy the moment to its fullest. My mind was clear of worries, and I had not a care in the world. *What a great feeling.* I dozed off for a few minutes and was awakened by the sound of Peter's voice.

"Hey, hon, there's Scott."

I looked up to see Scott running on the beach. I waved, but he didn't notice me. The same security guard we had met a day earlier was standing in attention. He too had seen Scott sprinting towards him. Soon, the two of them were engaged in an animated conversation. Scott was gesturing wildly while the security guard looked perplexed from what I could surmise from my vantage point.

Obviously, something was wrong, and I could not help thinking that it was about Julia.

"Peter, what's with Scott? They've been talking for quite a while. Scott seems really distraught. I think we should go see what's going on."

"I don't know what's happening…I'm concerned too. But I don't want us to get involved."

"But, don't you think Scott could use some support?"

"That's nice of you, Misty, but I don't want you to get upset with other people's problems."

"Get upset about what? We don't even know what's going on. Let's find out and try to help if we can. I thought you liked him?"

"Look, Misty, you have been so stressed at work for months and you're finally starting to let loose and relax here. We only have one week of R&R before the daily grind starts all over again. You don't need to add to your worries. You don't need that now."

"Peter, I appreciate where you're coming from, but we don't even know what it's all about. I'm going over there now to find out." I stood up and put my beach wrap around my waist and leaned over to put my flip-flops on.

"NO!" barked Peter.

The couple relaxing beside us looked up and stared at us. Peter waved and smiled to reassure them.

I was not just astounded, I was furious. And when I replied to Peter in a barely audible voice, he was stunned by the firmness of my tone. "Peter, don't raise your voice to me again."

"Fine, you stay here, and I'll go over to see what's going on," Peter barked and stormed off.

Peter left me fuming. He had never yelled at me before. *Why is he acting that way? What's wrong with him?*

It was a good fifteen minutes before Peter came back to report to me. His demeanor had changed. He no longer looked irritated. I could see the tension on his face. Something was going on that did not look right. It did not go well, I thought.

"What's going on, Peter?"

"Scott is convinced that Julia is missing, and he's asking the security guard to call the police."

"Oh my god! What makes him believe that?"

"Well, last night he surprisingly took my advice and left a message with the concierge asking Julia to contact him to let him know that she was okay. He also taped a note to her door with the same message. As of this morning she has not yet contacted him, and the note is still on her door. The concierge has not seen her either."

"It does seem odd that none of us have seen her since yesterday. I mean, it's a tiny resort, and we keep bumping into the same people all the time. Surely, there's a good explanation for why we can't find her. Maybe she went on a trip into town?"

"There's more," said Peter.

I swallowed hard, waiting for him to continue.

"When Scott went by Julia's room today, the maid was cleaning the room across the hallway. He asked her to open Julia's room to see if she was inside. The maid knocked, and when no one answered, she went in to check the room. Scott said he could see from the doorway that the room was cleaned, and the bed was made. There were a few pieces of luggage and some clothes on the chair. He saw Julia's cell phone on the nightstand in her room. He asked the maid if she had just cleaned the room, and she said she did not need to clean the room because it had not been used."

I could sense a familiar anxious feeling rising inside of me. My heart and mind began racing…

What if she had a friend here and had spent the night off the resort? But why would she leave her phone behind? I gasped for air. A coughing spell followed. A sure sign that I was about to have an anxiety attack.

Peter noticed right away that all was not well with me. I could hear the distress in his voice as he leaned forward and said, "Take long deep breaths, sweetheart. Inhale and exhale slowly, take your time."

Peter was gently holding onto me in his arms. After a short spell, my breathing came back to normal, and slowly I was able to recover my composure. But I was annoyed at myself for not better controlling my emotions. I should know better, particularly when I could sense that an anxiety spike was coming. Peter had kept a close watch on me all that time. He was staring into my eyes, which made me feel uncomfortable.

"I'm fine now, Peter."

"Thank God. This is exactly why I don't want you to get involved. You can't handle it."

"I'm fine, Peter! You can't always shelter me. Please tell me what else you found out."

Peter gave a long sigh. I crossed my arms waiting for his response.

"Scott and the security guard are going to speak to the manager of the resort right now before they talk to the police."

"Peter, we have to help find her."

"*No*! It's not a good idea! It's not our business! Look at what just happened to you. Let the police take care of it."

I absolutely hated the way he was speaking to me. "Why are you shouting at me?" Now it was my turn to raise my voice.

"I told you before, it's our vacation, and we don't need any more stress in our lives, especially you. Let the professionals handle it. It's what they do," he retorted.

"You're being insensitive."

"I'm being reasonable. There's nothing we can do."

"But..."

"Leave it alone, Misty!" Peter shouted, attempting to put an end to our discussion.

I did not know how to respond, so I remained silent. I understood what he was trying to do, but he was going about it the wrong way. It was infuriating. He should have known that I don't like to be told what to do. Even less being yelled at. It just raised my blood pressure and my anxiety levels. Him screaming at me served no real purpose. He should know that by now. I wanted to help find Julia. That was all. I made up my mind that I was going to do just that. Too bad for Peter. He did not need to know. I stared at Peter, who was standing in front of me with his arms crossed. It looked like a standoff. That's when I finally decided to put my foot down.

I wiped my face and took an invisible deep breath. "Peter, I find your behavior very upsetting. I really need to go back to the room and be by myself. Please don't follow me."

"Look, Misty, I'm upset too, and don't take me wrong, I care about Scott and Julia. But I care about you much more." He took a deep breath to calm himself down. "Go back to the room if you want. I'll be here if you need me."

Peter had made a conciliatory gesture in order not to exacerbate the situation any further. I stood still for a while, mulling my next step. Without a word, I grabbed my things and headed back to our room. I sat on the bed and took a moment to process what had just happened. Thoughts of Peter, Julia, and Scott came all at once rushing into my mind. Julia was my main concern at this point. My first instinct was to try to help find her and offer support to Scott. But Peter was adamant that I stay out of it. I could not stand another argument with him, which made me nervous and apprehensive. Anguishing about all these things was not helpful. On cue, I felt the onset of another anxiety attack coming again, and I remembered that I had forgotten to bring my medication on the trip. Peter had asked me on the flight if the meds were in my carry-on bag. "Of course, sweetheart." I had lied to him. I didn't want him to worry about me. I suddenly had a hard time breathing. My heart was pounding in my chest. I closed my eyes and tried to control my breathing and slow down my heartbeat. I feared the onset of a full-blown panic attack if I didn't calm myself down quickly. *I've got to overcome it without my medication. I must be strong.*

I was aware that I worry too much. But worrying alone was not the root cause of my condition. I was convinced that problems left unattended for a long time would end up consuming anyone. It was the fear of a prolonged, or worse, a lack of any resolution, that worried me to death. Now was the time to put away my fears, if I wanted to control my surging anxiety attack.

It took me a long time to restore my normal breathing and chase away all my negative thoughts. I was so proud of myself and although I was feeling tired, I still felt compelled to talk to Scott and the manager of the resort. Peter would not be happy, but there was no stopping me. I inhaled a satisfying deep breath and headed for the main lobby of the resort. On the way there, I passed Julia's room. Scott's note for Julia to call him was still affixed to the door. That the note was left untouched made me even more determined to go ahead with my plan.

In the lobby, I found the concierge partially hidden behind the front desk playing games on his phone. The reception area was empty. There were no check-ins or departures scheduled at that time.

The concierge put down his phone the moment he heard me approach the front desk. "How can I help you, miss?" he asked.

"Can I speak to the manager?"

"He's in a meeting now, but you're welcome to wait here. Or I can try to help."

"No, thank you. I'll wait," I said as I looked for a place to sit.

"The manager's office is around the corner. He asked not to be disturbed, but when he's available I'll let him know you wish to speak to him. What's your name, miss?"

"Misty."

I waited anxiously for what seemed like an hour. Then I saw Scott emerge from around the corner of the front desk. He looked awful. I immediately got up and went straight to him.

"Is there any news?"

"No. I've asked resort management to alert the police."

"What did they say?"

"They tried to reassure me at first, but in the end, they agreed to call the police."

"Scott, what can I do to help?"

"Misty, there's nothing you can do. But I appreciate your offer."

"Do you have a picture of her on your phone?" I asked.

"Yes, I already gave it to the manager, and he will share it with the police."

"Could you text it to me so that I can ask around?"

"Look, Misty, again, I appreciate you're trying to help, but I think it would be best if we leave it to the police." It was not the response I was expecting. I stood my ground pointing at his phone. He didn't budge.

"Look, Misty, sorry, but I have to go. Can we touch base later?"

Once again, I insisted. "Sure, but let's exchange numbers. so we can be in touch in case one of us finds out something."

Scott finally gave in, texted me his phone number, and rushed off. I couldn't understand why he did not want me to get involved. What was the harm in that? As I watched him hurry away the thought of Peter crept into my mind. I had to get back to our room in case he was looking for me. *Knowing him, he'll freak out if he can't find me.* That was the last thing I needed at the moment.

I hurried along the main lobby, heading for the walkway at the center of the main courtyard. Slightly out of breath, I reached the point where the walkway split into two lanes that symmetrically wound around the pool deck. The right way was the quickest way to get to the room. I was about to take the right turn when I spotted Peter talking to Scott at the opposite end of the walkway. I stopped to take a good look at them, infuriated about what I thought they were discussing. *Now Peter will know that I'm still trying to get involved in Julia's disappearance.* I was left with no choice but to get back to the room and get ready for another showdown with Peter. "This time it will be different," I swore under my breath while running as fast as I could.

I froze in fear at the threshold of the door. A gigantic crab was staring at me with its dreadful protruding black eyes. I tried to shoo it away, but it refused to cooperate. I took a step back, fearing an attack by this creature. With so many legs, how could I know which way it would go? I loved nature and animals in general, but I did not trust beings that could move in any direction on a whim. "Get out of my way!" I shouted at it.

"Misty! What's wrong?" Peter suddenly appeared from around the corner of the hallway.

"Peter!" I screamed back.

Peter seemed puzzled. "What's going on? Why are you yelling?"

"I was yelling at the big-eyed monster!"

"What big-eyed monster?"

"The huge crab. Didn't you see it?"

Peter stared at me incredulously. I looked around, searching for the crab. But the crab was gone. "It was there a second ago, believe me." I checked the door behind me in the hallway, but I could not find any trace of the damn creature.

"Are you okay, Misty?" Peter asked, looking somewhat concerned.

I took a deep breath and managed to get a hold of my nerves. "Well, yes, I think so…"

"Where were you? I came back looking for you earlier, but you weren't in the room."

"I…umm…I went for a walk. I wasn't able to sleep," I lied.

"Oh?"

"Yes, I just went for a long walk around the grounds and then went to the lobby to check out the gift shop. Then I bumped into Scott."

"I just saw Scott as well. I guess he told you that the resort management is going to report Julia's absence to the police."

"Yes, he did," I replied. But what I really wanted to say was, *"I wish we could do something to help."* I bit my tongue instead knowing that would provoke Peter. Besides, we needed to have a serious talk about the way things were going between us. But now was not the time. I was in no condition for another argument.

"Look, Misty, the situation with Julia is disturbing, I grant you that. But it's a small island and I'm sure the police will find her. In the meantime, let's try to chill by the pool for a while. It'll do us good. We need to cool things off between us."

I pretended to agree, not fully convinced that all would be fine with Julia. I gathered our towels and headed to the pool with Peter, thinking that it was probably an ideal place to be. It was in the middle of the resort property, and we could easily spot Scott or Julia if they went by. We placed our towels on the lounge chairs in our usual spot under the shade of a large umbrella. Peter didn't waste any time and went for a quick dip in the pool. I tried to take my mind off Julia by continuing my read of *Nomad on the Run*. To my surprise, I was somewhat successful with the welcome distraction. I finished a chapter when the heat started to make me feel uncomfortable. Meanwhile, Peter had returned from his swim and was looking for his bag where he had tossed his phone. I told him I was going for a dip in the pool to cool myself off, but I don't think he heard me. He was already distracted by his phone.

The water was a welcome refreshing break, and I decided to do some laps to get rid of the remnants of tension in my body. I completed several laps and only paused to avoid collisions with other swimmers. When I was satisfied with my workout, I swam to the edge of the infinity pool, which overlooked the beach. The azure waters were crystal clear, a beautiful contrast against the very fine white sand. I no longer felt the intense tension that seemed to burden me most of the time. Exercise could always relieve my stress. I discovered its healing power after many hard days at the office. It was like a cleanse of body and mind. *What a privilege to be here. If I were back home in Toronto right now, I would be at my desk, dealing with the routine grind and toxic environment.* The workplace culture was not good for my health. I had known it ever since the takeover by our foreign parent company but never truly admitted it to myself. I kept thinking the working conditions would get better with time. I was wrong. The answer seemed obvious. I just refused to accept it. The passage of time made things even worse.

I stepped out of the pool and noticed Scott talking to Peter. I immediately thought that something must be happening,

"Is there any news?" I blurted, out of breath from my swim.

"No. The local police came to the resort and wanted to talk to anyone who had any contact with Julia. Would you both be willing to speak to the police and answer a few routine questions?" Scott asked.

"Of course, It's the least we could do!" I volunteered right away.

Peter did not look too happy. "Scott, I don't think we have any useful information to offer. We barely know her. I mean, we only spoke to Julia a few brief times."

"Hey bud, I know you're on vacation, but it will just take a few minutes. I would really appreciate you taking the time."

I nudged Peter, "Come on, hon, we need to do something to help. Let's go talk to the police." I put on my beach wrap and grabbed my bag. Peter followed begrudgingly.

At the main lobby, Peter and I were asked by the resort manager to wait in a small conference room adjacent to his office. We left Scott pacing outside the door. After a few minutes, two police officers entered the room. They introduced themselves as officers Javier and Juan and sat down across the table from us.

"Do you recognize the lady in this picture?" The officer showed us a picture of Julia and Scott, taken the night of my birthday. In the photo, Scott looked happy and had his arm wrapped around Julia's shoulder. They were both seated at a dining table. Julia looked more serious. She was not smiling. It was hard to tell if she was uncomfortable or just shy. But she looked naturally beautiful with very little make-up. She wore a delicate red scarf that was loosely hung around her neck. The officers asked a few more questions about how we met Julia and if she mentioned any plans about leaving the resort.

"When did you last see Julia?" Officer Juan asked.

I looked at Peter and answered, "It was two days ago. I remember because it was the day of my birthday. I had a brief conversation with her on the beach."

"What did you talk about?"

"Nothing much, really. She didn't seem to be in the mood to chat, so I excused myself after a few minutes."

"What about you, Peter? When was the last time you saw Julia?"

Peter was silent for a few moments and seemed uptight when he spoke. "I saw her in the late evening after we celebrated Misty's birthday."

I was confused by Peter's answer. I didn't remember seeing Julia that evening, and Peter and I were together the whole time.

"What time did you last see her that evening?" The officer asked Peter, taking note of my reaction.

"It had to be around 11:30 p.m., probably closer to midnight. I walked Misty to our room after a late dinner around eleven. We were going to have drinks on the terrace adjacent to our room, but Misty was too tired and fell asleep right away."

Peter paused for a moment, looked at me briefly, saw the shock on my face, and then continued, "I didn't feel like staying in the room, so I went to the beach bar to grab a beer. There was a little celebration going on because the Leafs had just won a playoff game. I remember seeing Julia pass by the bar, and I yelled out her name. She didn't hear me and kept walking towards the beach."

"Was she alone?" Juan asked.

"Yes, she was alone."

"How long did you stay at the bar?"

"Maybe for an hour or so."

"Did you see her after that?"

"No, I never saw her again."

Peter looked annoyed by all the questions. He suddenly stood up, and his voice rose along with him, "Are we done here?" He grumbled while staring down at the policemen.

Officer Juan rubbed his chin, briefly looked at his partner and then took a quick glance at me. He did not seem entirely satisfied with Peter's answers, but I guess he decided to let it go for the time being. "Yes, thank you, sir. That will be all for now."

Peter left the room abruptly and didn't even wait for me. I got up right away and rushed after him. Scott stopped me on the way out. He had been waiting for us in the lobby.

"Misty!"

"Scott, sorry, I didn't see you there."

"Is Peter alright? He walked right past me, like he was in a big hurry."

"Yeah, he's alright. I think he was worried someone would snag our spot by the pool." I tried to cover for him. But deep down, I was really disturbed. *He never mentioned anything about seeing Julia that night? Why?*

"Misty, what did the cops say? Do they have any ideas about where Julia could be?" Scott asked.

"They asked routine questions about how we know Julia and when we last saw her." I hesitated to ask Scott what was on my mind but, after a short deliberation, thought better of it and plunged right into it. "Hey Scott, you know the night of my birthday? Well, I just found out that Peter went to the beach bar after I fell asleep and saw Julia walk by. Do you know anything about that?"

"What? Really? I walked her to her room just after ten. She said she was tired and barely said good night to me. I assumed she was going to sleep for the night. Why would she go to the beach by herself so late at night? That doesn't make any sense!"

"Maybe she couldn't sleep?" I tried to offer a logical explanation, but Scott did not look convinced. I did not blame him for doubting.

"Sorry, Scott, I need to catch up with Peter, let me know if you hear anything. You have my number. Text me anytime."

"Thanks, Misty. And sorry if speaking to the police has caused you or Peter any stress."

Peter and I definitely need to have a serious talk.

I stepped outside looking for Peter. The sun was blaring over my head. Forbidding, not inviting, like a warning not to pursue my search. The beach was virtually deserted, most guests had gathered under the protection of large umbrellas surrounding the pool. I hesitated for a moment. Was it the right time to confront Peter? I thought better of it and hurried to the pool area. All the best shaded spots had been snatched. The lounge chairs we had occupied earlier had been taken by an elderly couple. The heat was getting to me. It all seemed pointless. I felt dizzy and almost gave up my search when I finally found him at a table at the perimeter of the pool area. He was sitting with a beer in his hand under a blistering sun, which was unusual for him. I could see that he was preoccupied with something he was reading on his phone. I approached him from behind and put my hand on his shoulder.

"Hey, you," I said.

He jumped up from his seat, clearly annoyed. "Don't sneak up on me from behind like that!"

"Sorry, Peter. Is everything okay? You left so suddenly. I was concerned about you."

"You know how I feel about getting involved in other people's business," he said curtly.

"I know, but how could we say no to helping someone in trouble?"

"Look, we did our duty, and there's nothing more we can do. We're here for a week, and we only have a few full days left. Let them be for us to enjoy, okay?"

"No, it's not okay. What really happened out there, Peter?"

"What do you mean?"

"You stormed out of the room."

"As I said, I'd had enough of the meaningless questions. The police were just going through the motions."

"They have a job to do."

"Well, let them do it."

"When were you going to tell me?"

"Tell you what?"

"Don't play games with me, Peter."

"As I said, you were asleep, and I didn't feel like staying in the room."

"What else happened?"

"Are you accusing me of something? Are you suspicious?"

"I'm not suspicious. I'm curious."

"Nothing happened, Misty. I'd a beer or two, saw Julia walking by, and then went back to our room."

"I wished you had told me that earlier."

"There was nothing to tell."

At that point, I thought it was best to be agreeable and end the discussion. Besides, I was not fully recovered from my recent anxiety onset. It would take time. Patience was required. I was bothered by Peter's behavior and the fact that he had kept his encounter with Julia a secret from me. But I knew there would be a more opportune time to sort out our differences.

While Peter was preoccupied with his phone, I took this opportunity to go for another quick swim. Unfortunately, no matter how hard and how long I kept at it, it did not do much to relieve the awful apprehension that was rising inside of me. *Damn it! Why did I not bring my meds with me?* Tired but still anxious, I found a lounge chair that had just been vacated. I grabbed my towel and laid it on the chair. I needed to clear my mind and not let the interaction with Peter bother me anymore. I tried to focus on being in the moment, concentrating on my breathing, one breath at a time. I let the hot Caribbean sun warm my face, and the light breeze brush my skin. I envisioned the waves in the ocean and recalled their calming rhythm. I made myself aware of all the soothing sensations caressing my face, body, and mind. And I gradually began to relax while breathing slowly and keeping my eyes shut.

I was drifting…I imagined that I was floating on my back in the ocean, allowing the waves to take me on a ride far away from the shore. I let my body sink slowly in the water without panic or fear. I opened my eyes and was mesmerized by vivid colors, exotic plants, and schools of fish. I saw sea turtles swimming around me, and I decided to follow them. There were maybe four or five of them, and they were guiding me to the bottom of the ocean. *But why were they swimming so fast? I thought turtles were slow.* They swiftly led me to some tangled piece of cloth that was wrapped around one turtle's neck and snagged onto a deep-rooted sea plant at the other end. The turtles wanted my help. I swam down to the plant and tried to loosen the knot. I struggled but finally set the little sea turtle free. The turtles swam circles around me, as if to thank me, and then left me alone underwater. I suddenly realized I needed to come up for air. I panicked and frantically swam up to the surface. I made it just in time. I gasped and struggled to catch my breath. I looked at my hand. I was still clenching the material fragment, which had trapped and almost strangled the sea turtle. I opened my grip and saw a piece of fabric that looked familiar. I screamed, and I woke up to find Peter comforting me.

"Hon... it's ok. You were having a nightmare."

"What?"

"You dozed off, and you were screaming in your sleep."

"I think she drowned."

"Who?"

"Julia."

"Why would you think that?"

"Remember when we were on the glass bottom boat tour? I saw a scarf tangled on a dock post underwater. I believe it was the same scarf Julia wore in the picture with Scott, taken that night she was last seen."

Peter rolled his eyes. "Misty, you had a bad dream."

"But Peter, I know what I saw. It was Julia's scarf, I'm sure of it."

"Perhaps you're right. But if it was Julia's scarf that you saw, that doesn't mean Julia drowned. She could simply have lost it in the water. It's very windy on the island. The scarf might have flown away with the wind and landed in the ocean."

"But it's too much of a coincidence."

At this point, Peter had lost it. He leaned over me and snapped. "You know what all this is telling me? That you're anxious, which is exactly why you needed a vacation in the first place. You obsess about things to the point your anxiety takes over. And then you stop thinking clearly. Let this one go. It's not our job to play detective. I sincerely hope they find Julia, but you need to relax!"

No longer able to contain myself, I felt anger swelling up inside of me. "On this one Peter, I don't agree with you!"

Peter grabbed his phone and wallet from the table, put on his shirt, and stormed off. He never said where he was going, and I didn't ask.

It was a good thing that he left me alone. The way the conversation had ended was not only a big disappointment, it also made me want to reevaluate everything about our relationship. Peter was right about one thing though. I needed to do a better job of controlling my anxiety. So, I slipped into the pool and did some laps. I came out feeling better. I dried myself off and sat back down in the lounge chair. I flipped through a celebrity magazine to try to distract myself from how annoyed I was about the whole situation. *Why does he get so angry with me? He knows it's in my nature to try to help others. He doesn't need to raise his voice at me. It makes me feel like a child.* I flipped angrily through the glossy pages. I stopped at a picture that caught my eye. It was an advertisement for a moisturizer. The model had flawless skin, of course, and had a scarf loosely wrapped around her neck. It made me think of the picture of Julia and the scarf that I saw underwater on the glass bottom boat tour. *I must do something about it. I'm sure that it's Julia's scarf.* I reached for my phone and texted Scott. I told Scott to check out the scarf underwater by the dock where the glass bottom boat and the water taxis were moored.

I felt good about myself. Too many times I had held myself back from doing what I thought was right out of fear. It was true that I worry too much, and perhaps far too much for my own good, but that should not stop me. I sat back on the lounge chair and shut my eyes. I had no idea how long Peter had been gone, but when I opened my eyes, I saw him hovering over me. He had brought me cold lemon water and seemed to have calmed down.

"Please drink, it'll make you feel better."

I could tell that he was feeling guilty, and this was his way to make amends. I appreciated the gesture and drank a sip of water. But I was still not ready to forgive him for the way he had treated me. I had never tolerated this behavior from anyone. *Why should I do that now?*

"You were gone for a while, where did you go?" I curtly said.

"I booked a day tour of the island on the next available date, the day after tomorrow. I think you'll love it."

"Oh? I don't know if I'm up for a long day out in this heat."

"We'll visit a chocolate factory, a rum cake shop, and have lunch on a secluded beach.

Look, Misty, this is a small resort, and I think we could use a change of scenery."

I folded my arms, waiting to hear more. I could see that he was really trying hard to please me, and in his own way, trying to make amends. I was touched, even if I hated myself for giving in so easily. I smiled knowing that his heart was in the right place. Besides, I could not bear another disagreement.

"Is that your beautiful smile I see? That means yes? All is cool between us?"

I laughed and reached for his hand and gave it a squeeze. "Peter, that sounds wonderful, thank you for arranging it."

"I'm very sorry about what happened earlier. I didn't mean to snap at you. It's just...that I love you so much, and I hate to see you get all worked up. You know what that does to you."

"I know, Peter. You mean well, but sometimes you can be overbearing. I know you have the best intentions and want to protect me. But sometimes the way you go about it just makes it worse. Let me be me. Don't worry so much. Anyway, the sun will be setting soon. Let's go back to our room, shower, and change. A walk along the beach before dinner is exactly what we both need."

"Sounds wonderful."

He leaned forward and gave me a passionate kiss. I kissed him back hard.

Some things are just better than talking.

CHAPTER 6

"Anxiety was born in the very same moment as mankind. And since we will never be able to master it, we will have to learn to live with it—just as we have learned to live with storms."

—Paulo Coelho

Unfortunately, my serious talk with Peter would have to wait for another time. I was on my way to join Peter, who had saved a seat for me by the pool, when a police officer approached me in the lobby. He looked barely twenty-years-old in his immaculate uniform. He stood in front of me and raised his right hand to stop me. I was about to protest when

I finally recognized him as the other policeman who took notes while Officer Juan was questioning us in the resort's conference room.

"Ma'am, Officer Juan would like to have a word with you, please follow me."

"Where to?"

"Officer Juan is waiting for you at the police station."

"Why can't he come over here to talk to me?"

"Ma'am, you must understand Officer Juan is on desk duty. We are a small police force, and someone must man the station at all times."

"What is this all about? Does it have anything to do with Julia?"

"My car is parked nearby, please come with me. I'm sure Officer Juan will fully brief you."

"Give me a second, please. I'd like to call my boyfriend to let him know where I'm going."

The police officer took a step back and glanced at his watch. That gesture served only to raise my anxiety level that was about to explode. I fumbled with my phone and after a few deep breaths, I finally managed to settle my nerves enough to call Peter.

"Hey, Misty, where are you? You should feel how warm the water is in the pool. It's heavenly!"

"Listen, Peter. I can't talk to you right now. I'm on my way to the police station. Officer Juan sent me a car. He wants to see me....No, I don't know what it's all about."

"Misty..."

"Peter, I'll talk to you when I get back."

The winding road was barely wide enough for two small cars to pass by without incident. On several occasions we had to quickly swerve to the side of the road to let the large trucks and buses bolt past us. The young cop at the wheel seemed to know what he was doing, which was somewhat reassuring. But his constant use of the horn every time a vehicle drove by was giving me a headache—let alone what it did to my blood pressure. During the entire ride I clenched my teeth and kept my arms crossed in front of me. It must have taken nearly an hour to get to Coxen Hole, the capital of Roatan, where I assumed we would find the police station.

Probably sensing my unease, the policeman looked up at the rearview mirror and told me that we were almost at the station. With a deep sigh of relief, I took the opportunity to take a peek outside the window. The city streets were clean, full of local merchants busily going about their day, sweeping the sidewalk in front of their vividly colored storefronts. No one seemed to be in a big hurry, people were chatting away at anyone who happened to pass by, and happy faces were everywhere. I liked what I saw and made a point of coming back with Peter to enjoy this city's charm.

The police station was a small, unassuming yellow building near the central park area on the outskirts of Coxen Hole. We parked alongside the only other police car and proceeded to enter the building. The police quarters were on the second floor, at the far end of a long hallway next to the offices of the Chief Justice. The front desk was occupied by a middle-aged woman and two or three empty cubicles on either side of her desk, constituted the entire reception area.

Officer Juan appeared from one of the corner offices and waved at me to join him.

Here it comes! Good news or bad news?

The office was small, plain, and clearly not meant to be welcoming. The rectangular wooden desk, three chairs that could have been bought at IKEA, and a tall metal coat hanger in the far end corner of the room, suggested a taste for functionality rather than comfort. The ultra-modern and probably very expensive computer with two very large curved screens sitting at opposite ends of the desk seemed so ill-suited in the otherwise unassuming office.

Officer Juan turned off the computer the moment I stepped in the office.

"Good morning, Misty. Please come in and have a seat. Coffee, water, or juice, perhaps?"

"No, thank you, I ate a copious breakfast at the resort." I was not about to let him know how I was really feeling. Something about this set up told me that it was best to remain guarded.

"I must first apologize for taking time away from your vacation. Unfortunately, I'm stuck behind my desk today."

Officer Juan's tone did not strike me as very apologetic. "You could have called me?"

Officer Juan let a hint of a smile slip on his lips. He ignored my remark and instead changed the subject.

"How long have you and Peter been dating?"

"Less than a year. Why the question? What does that have to do with Julia's disappearance? Do you think Peter is involved?"

"No, no, Misty. You've got it wrong. You see, Peter is the last person who saw Julia before her disappearance."

"And?"

"I was able to confirm that he was at the beach bar that night, like he said. A waitress and the barman did indeed remember him having a drink alone."

"Well, that's what he told you."

"The only sticking point, Misty, is that no one saw Julia near the bar that night."

"Do you suspect Peter of lying?"

Officer Juan let a second or two pass while staring at me. *He was a close observer*, I thought, *not a talker*. I felt very uncomfortable not knowing where this whole conversation was heading. I tried hard to maintain my composure and stared back at the officer to hide my discomfort. I did not flinch, proud that I had managed to keep my arising anxiety in check. Finally, Officer Juan broke away from his stare and looked down at a notepad on his desk, thought for a moment and said, "What did Peter tell you happened that night?"

"Exactly what he told you. I fell asleep after dinner, and he went to the beach bar for a nightcap. That's when he saw Julia walk by."

"Did he tell you anything else?"

"Like what?"

"Did he talk to her? Did he walk with her? Did he see anyone following her?"

I appraised him with a stern gaze. "Why are you asking me these questions? Why don't you talk to Peter?"

"I will, I will, Misty. I thought you might have some answers for me. Besides that's not the only reason I brought you here. There's another matter I would like to discuss with you. You strike me as a really nice lady, and I think you should know something about Scott Morrison's background."

At the mention of Scott's name, my heart started racing as my thoughts jumped all over the place. I was certain that Officer Juan was about to reveal something that would validate my mistrust. I sat back in the chair full of anticipation and waited for him to speak again.

"Tell me, how well do you know Scott?"

I chose my words carefully. "Not very well, I'm afraid. We just met him at the resort."

"As part of our investigation, we did a background check on him, and we found out…"

"Wait a minute. Are you checking up on Peter and me as well?"

"That's my job, Misty."

"I see. There seems to be a lack of trust here. What about Scott?"

"His record shows that he had a restraining order placed against him by a former girlfriend. She claimed verbal abuse and felt threatened, but upon further investigation, the order was rescinded."

"Why are you telling me this?"

"As a courtesy, Misty. I know you and Peter are hanging around with him. What's the expression—'Where there's smoke, there's fire.' Just keep this tip in the back of your mind. That's all."

Now I was intrigued.

My mind immediately went into high gear trying to decipher the real meaning, and more importantly the implications of what Officer Juan had just told me. Was it intended as a simple heads-up or something grimmer, like a warning? What about Peter? Was he holding back some dark secret from me? At the very least, I was perturbed by the whole conversation and by the way it was conducted in a police station. I had to admit Officer Juan was more cunning than I was giving him credit. *Plant a few seeds of doubt here and there, and wait to see what shakes up.* Unfortunately, if that was his intent, I was afraid that he might have succeeded.

"Is there anything else you want to tell me?" I asked exasperated.

"No. The policeman who brought you here will chauffeur you back. Thank you again for agreeing to meet me in my office."

The drive back to the resort started out as a smooth and uneventful ride. The morning rush hour had subsided and mercifully the driver had made little use of the car horn. I was about to lighten my hold of the armrest when all of the sudden the sky turned pitch black. A tropical storm had erupted above us and not long after the car, which was moving by that time at a crawl, stopped abruptly in a jerking motion.

"Sorry, ma'am, but the windshield wipers are no match for this downpour. It's too dangerous to drive under these conditions. There's a small coffee shop across the road, and I suggest we wait out the storm in there."

The idea of walking across the road in the middle of a tempest did not exactly sound like an appealing proposition. I glanced a couple of times at the window. It was a deluge out there, and I was barely able to see a few meters away. The wind had picked up, which made the torrential rain even more frightening. The young policeman noticed my hesitation and smiled at me.

"Ma'am, you can stay in the car if you want. I'll go get you a cup of coffee. Please, just stay put."

It would have stayed in the car if it were not for the loud and constant drum beat of the rain on the rooftop, and the car shaking widely under a gale force wind. I peeked outside one more time, feeling caught under two equally unpalatable choices.

The driver read my mind and said, "Ma'am, they have excellent coffee, and their pastries are even more delicious. You'll be more comfortable in the coffee shop."

"Alright, let's go," I said, not too convincingly.

We made a dash across the road. Drenched and out of breath, we entered the coffee shop and grabbed the first available table. The place smelled of strong coffee and indeed the pastry trays lined up on the countertop looked very, very appetizing. The coffee shop was modestly decorated and full of patrons. It was obviously a popular place possessing a warmth that emanated pride and loving care by its owner. My escort noticed me staring at the flag hanging above the cash register.

"The owner is a Canadian expat. Many tourists come here on vacation and fall in love with the island. There's a large expat community in Roatan. Maybe you'll be tempted to move to Roatan one day?"

I rolled my eyes in response. His timing was completely off. There was a long awkward silence between us as we kept our eyes down on our plates. Then over a second cup of coffee and a cookie in the shape of a maple leaf, he asked if I was feeling better.

"What do you think? A guest at the resort has vanished, no one knows what happened to her, and then the island gets blown off by a hurricane."

"Ma'am, it's not a…"

"Stop calling me ma'am, my name is Misty."

"I'm sorry, ma'am, I mean, Misty. I didn't mean to offend you. We don't get hurricanes in Roatan. This is just a bad tropical storm. It'll blow over quickly, you'll see."

"Let's hope so."

"Misty, I know you are upset that your friend has not yet been found. Believe me when I tell you this. Officer Juan will not stop working on the case until it's solved. He is stubborn that way."

"I do hope you're right. But so far, I've not seen any evidence of it."

"You will. Believe me. He is the best we have."

"We'll see," I said, far from being convinced. "But I think it stopped raining. Let's get going if you don't mind."

A crowd had gathered in the main lobby when I arrived. It seemed every guest in the resort had the same idea and sought refuge from the rain in the cramped lobby. I looked around for Peter, but I could not find him among the hordes of people. I made a right turn heading for our room, and that was when I finally spotted him leaning against the wall with his phone in hand.

Always the phone.

"When did you get back?" he asked when he saw me coming his way.

"Just a few minutes ago. What a storm, eh?"

"So, what did he want from you?"

"Not much really. He wanted to update me on his search…nothing particularly significant though."

"Are you telling me that he made you go all the way over there to tell what…nothing?"

"I guess he felt the need to show me that he's working hard on the case. I don't know, Peter."

"Misty, I know you're not telling me everything."

"Peter, please don't start. Listen, I don't think the police have any idea where she could possibly be. There's one thing though, he wants to talk to you."

"What about?"

"Just a matter of going over what happened the night you saw Julia near the beach bar."

"But I already told him everything I know."

"He wants to hear it again, I suppose. Is there anything else you forgot to tell him?"

"No, Misty. What are you getting at?"

"Nothing, Peter. Everything is cool. By the way, have you heard from Scott?"

"It's funny you should ask. I've been looking for him all morning, but I have no clue where he could possibly be."

"Have you tried knocking at his door?"

"Yeah, no luck there either."

"He couldn't be too far. You'll find him. Let's go for a walk. The sun just came out."

"Yeah, sure. Are you still up to our trip off the resort tomorrow?"

"Absolutely! We both need a good distraction."

Escapism, at times, can be helpful.

CHAPTER 7

"Just when the caterpillar thought the world was ending, he turned into a butterfly."

—Anonymous

*W*e woke up the next day to another blissful morning with a clear blue sky. We sipped coffee on the terrace until it was time to meet our tour guide for our day trip. A small group of tourists adorned with sun hats, beach bags, and cameras had already assembled in the lobby area. The bus had not yet arrived, and we were all anxious to get going. Our tour guide looked at his phone a couple of times, and when he saw the bus turn the corner, he asked us to gather around him. He briefly introduced himself as he collected our tickets.

The tour bus was half full until the next stop at another resort nearby. After a short delay, allowing just enough time for the new passengers to board, the bus hit the only road that traversed the island from one end to the other. The ride was bumpy, but no one complained as our attention was drawn to the lush tropical forest that threatened to overcome the narrow winding road at any time.

Sitting beside me, Peter was quiet and rather subdued. He kept gazing out the window as if lost in thought. I felt the same way after what had transpired over the past couple of days. For both our sakes we badly needed a distraction. This excursion outside of the resort could not have come at a better time.

Our first destination was the butterfly conservatory. It was a large greenhouse filled with exotic plants, where butterflies flew freely. A lady in our group with a ridiculously large floppy hat screamed when some butterflies came close to her face. She chased them away and then insisted on taking a selfie while the butterflies were flying around at a safe distance. I observed her for a moment chuckling, and then wandered off on my own. I snapped close-up pictures of blossoming flowers covered with different kinds of multicolored butterflies. In the far corner of the conservatory, the tour guide was explaining to a small group that had gathered around him the full circle of life, from egg, larva, cocoon, to adult. I was sad to hear the average lifespan of an adult butterfly was only two weeks. I went on meandering around the greenhouse, completely captivated by the experience and oblivious to the fact that the group had moved outside to interact with the macaws. I looked for Peter but could not find him in the conservatory. So, I stepped outside where everyone had gathered around the macaws. In the middle of the group, the nervous lady with the floppy hat was fixing herself for a pose with one of the colorful birds. Despite the fact she was clearly afraid of the macaw, she wanted to be the first to have her picture taken with it. Peter and I exchanged a quick glance. He rolled his eyes, and I smiled.

I waited for my turn for a picture to be taken with the beautiful bird. I knew it was a cliché, but in the spirit of the moment, I thought why not, I'm a tourist after all, and I took my turn like all the other visitors. The tour guide put "Frisky" the macaw on my shoulder, and I gave my phone to Peter to snap a picture. He fiddled with the phone while I waited patiently, trying to hold onto my pose. Frisky was getting fidgety, and I was getting tired.

Laughing out loud I said, "Hurry up, hon, I'm afraid the bird might make a nest in my hair."

"Sorry, Misty, your phone battery just died, and I left my phone at the resort. I thought we needed to unplug for a day at least."

I was so disappointed. The guide took the bird off my shoulder, thanked everyone for visiting the conservatory and then asked us to board the bus.

We were ready to leave when the guide realized we were missing one couple. After a good ten-minute wait, the lady with the floppy hat and her husband finally climbed onboard. "Sorry, sorry, bathroom break," she kept repeating while making her way to her seat. Peter looked annoyed and stared at the couple who had delayed us all. I nudged him and whispered, "If she was afraid of butterflies, I wonder how she'll be with the iguanas?"

The bus driver did not even wait for the couple to sit down as he hastily shut the door and drove off right away. After a short drive, the bus pulled up to the iguana farm. We were instructed that we could only feed the iguanas with the leaves provided by the staff. Peter and I descended onto the walkway where iguanas of all sizes cluttered the narrow road in front of us. We were quickly surrounded by a horde of hungry, prehistoric looking lizards waiting to be fed. I was surprised by how aggressive these giant lizards were chasing after their food. Meanwhile, not everyone managed to step outside, and we could hear some sort of commotion not far behind us on the bus. I looked inside the tour bus to see what was causing so much rau-cous. The lady with the floppy hat was arguing with her husband, yelling at him that she did not want to leave the bus because she was afraid of the iguanas. A couple of passengers at the back waiting to disembark were laughing at the lady, and Peter rolled his eyes at me once again.

"I don't understand why she's afraid of these docile creatures. They're harmless," said Peter.

"You can't control your fears, Peter. People should understand that instead of laughing at her. I feel sorry for her."

Peter went off to feed a large iguana while I went back to the bus to grab my sunglasses. The lady with the floppy hat was sitting alone in the back of the bus. Her husband had given up trying to convince her to get off the bus. She was holding onto her purse while peeking out the window at the iguanas roaming around on the road below her.

"Are you okay?" I asked. I looked into her eyes and could tell that the poor lady was genu-inely afraid.

"I'm terrified of iguanas!"

"There's really nothing to be afraid of. They do look a little scary, but really, they're totally harmless. They would never bring buses of tourists here if there was any danger."

To my surprise, she began to cry.

"I'm so sorry. I didn't mean to upset you, perhaps I'm not much help."

"My husband is so annoyed with me. He wants me to be more adventurous, and I am really trying... but this really scares me!" She said while wiping a tear from her cheek.

"I understand, but don't be so hard on yourself... We're all afraid of one thing or another. Do you want me to get your husband?"

"No, I don't want to spoil this for him. He's been looking forward to this trip. It's as much his holiday as it is mine."

"Look," I said, trying to reassure her. "The rest of the day tour will be much better. According to the itinerary, our next stop is the secluded beach where we'll have lunch, then the chocolate factory, and the rum cake shop. No more iguanas."

She stopped crying and said, "You had me with the chocolate factory." And we both shared a good laugh.

Our next stop was like a postcard picture. In front of us stretching for miles was a diamond white sand beach with palapas standing above crystal-clear aquamarine waters. Little French Key was everything the brochure had promised—a marvelous oasis of pristine beauty. I understood now why it was the favorite destination of the tourists that came to visit Roatan.

"Wow, Peter, isn't this beautiful!"

"Hey, don't ever complain that I don't take you to nice places!" I could tell that Peter was equally impressed.

We were told to gather on the dock where a flat pontoon boat was waiting to ferry us to a semi-deserted beach across the bay. We took our seats on the deck for the short ride to the beach. As the boat sailed on the calm water to our final destination, everyone kept quiet, taken by the beauty of the surroundings. Suddenly a woman screamed. We all turned around alarmed by what might be going on at the back of the boat. The lady who was afraid of the iguanas was standing up in the middle of the boat, pointing her finger at the water while shouting, "My hat! My hat!"

Peter turned to me and whispered, "What now?"

We looked in the distance and saw her floppy hat floating away with the current. A man on a small motorboat saw what had happened and tried to catch up with the hat, which was being pulled away by the strong undercurrent. We all watched the man making several attempts trying to catch the hat, missing every time he got close enough. At each failed attempt, the entire group sighed in unison, "Ohhhh!" The man kept circling back until he finally was able to scoop the hat out of the water. He raised the hat above his head in a triumphant pose, proud of himself. The group cheered, and everyone had a good laugh. After a while, the poor lady's husband grabbed his wife's wet hat, looking totally embarrassed by the whole misadventure.

The rest of the boat ride went smoothly to the relief of everyone onboard. About five minutes later, our pontoon reached the dock on the other side of the bay, where we would have lunch and spend the balance of the day on the beach.

"Oh, Peter, look how beautiful this place is! I'm so disappointed that my phone battery is dead. I'd love to take some pictures."

"Take pictures with your eyes, sweetheart. It's so much better."

"You're so right. I want to take it all in and remember this place forever. Let's go for a little walk along the beach and explore."

"You go ahead. I want to grab a beer at the bar and then head for one of those umbrella tables standing in the shallow water."

"Okay, I'll join you in a short while. I want to enjoy this paradise." I gave him a peck on the cheek and wandered off on my own.

I welcomed the opportunity to explore the immaculate beach of Little French Key. There was so much ground to cover, and I felt very safe being alone. I strolled along a wide dock where a number of brightly colored lounge chairs were lined up in a neat row facing the ocean. I was the only person on the dock, which surprised me. But it did not take me long to figure out the reason. It was simply too hot for anyone to spend any time on the dock. There was no shade or parasols to shield off the midday sun. Although the view from the dock was absolutely breathtaking, I regretfully left it behind me to head for a small inviting winding path I had spotted earlier. The path, which ended up being only a few meters in length, led to a small open area with two tall red wooden chairs, and just enough shade for only one couple to enjoy. The chairs gave way to a stunning view of the open waters. *I have to share this view with Peter.*

Our tour guide was standing nearby, puffing a cigarette and tapping on his cell phone. I startled him, and he quickly put his phone in his pocket.

"Hi there, sorry if I startled you."

"Hey, no problem." He smiled, recognizing me as one of his passengers on the bus. "Are you enjoying the tour?" he said in between a couple of quick puffs of his cigarette.

"Very much, thank you. This is indeed a very special place. This beach is a real gem. I'm so glad we ventured off the resort. I'm not complaining about our resort or its beach, mind you, they're absolutely wonderful. But this..." I stretched out my arms in a wide sweeping motion. "This, this...is truly awesome!"

The tour guide laughed. "Welcome to paradise!" He said in a deep and raspy voice. He was young and handsome and a bit of a flirt.

"The water seems so calm on the main beach, but here in the open water, it seems a little rough," I said.

"The currents are very strong around here, and the water is far too rough for swimming. That's why swimming is only permitted in the area over there." He pointed to the enclosed area where the umbrella tables were partially submerged in the water.

"That area is safe and shallow. It's kept calm from the current by the large rocks encircling the bay. But as you can see over there, there's a narrow opening. Every now and then a tourist gets curious and swims out beyond the limit. Past that opening, the underwater currents are very, very strong, and if they don't pull you from under and drown you, they will drag you out to the open sea where the waves will finish you off. No one can survive that. There have been a few bad accidents over the years. That's why I cautioned the group on our way here to stay within the confined area. In fact, my boss reminded me today to make sure to tell the group not to venture outside the designated safe area. There was an incident a couple of nights ago when a swimmer got into trouble out there."

"Oh no! Did the person make it back safely?"

"Don't really know. I was told that they pulled an unconscious person out of the water."

"Oh my God, that's terrible!"

"Yeah, just be careful, swim in the safe area, and everything will be fine, miss."

"I will, thanks. I better find out what my boyfriend is doing. Thanks again for the warning."

The tour guide smiled at me and gave me one thumbs up as he watched me leave.

I was troubled by what I'd learned, but I didn't want to dwell on it, remembering what Peter had told me earlier. *Don't worry so much.*

"Hey, hon!" Peter yelled as he saw me approach.

"Hey to you all!" I replied to acknowledge the group of fellow tourists who had joined Peter in the water. "So, this is where the party is taking place!"

By the looks of it, a sizable group had followed Peter's lead sitting around umbrella tables in the shallow end of the beach. The lady with the floppy hat and her husband had joined Peter at his table. They were all enjoying cold beers while soaking their feet in the water.

"How was your walk, hon?"

"A little too hot to enjoy, but I discovered a hidden gem of a spot that I want to share with you later, if we have time. This really is a special place." I made no mention of the drowning incident in keeping with my earlier resolution.

"I'll drink to that!" said the husband of the lady with the floppy hat while raising his half-empty glass in the air.

The four of us shared some light conversation about our travels. I was the only one not drinking alcohol, and I could tell our small group was already experiencing a bit of a buzz. They were getting loud and laughing a lot. They were having a good time. *I felt good*.

A little past noon, we heard the tour guide shouting from the restaurant at a distance, "Lunch will be served in fifteen minutes!"

"I wish we had more time here," said the lady with the floppy hat.

"I know what you mean. What an absolutely gorgeous beach. I wish I could take pictures of this paradise. Unfortunately, my phone is dead, and Peter didn't bring his, either."

"No problem, dear. I can take a few pictures after lunch and send them to you if you wish," said the lady with the floppy hat.

"Thank you, I would really appreciate that."

We all walked to the restaurant as a group and feasted on barbeque chicken, herbed rice, and grilled veggies. After lunch, we had a half hour of free time. Our new friends took some pictures for us. Then, I escorted Peter and the couple to the special hidden gem of a spot I'd discovered earlier. They were as amazed as I'd been. More pictures were taken of us as a group. Soon after, our visit to Little French Key ended.

After the short ferry ride back to the mainland, we boarded the bus, and the driver departed immediately. By now the group was a lot louder than when we first left for the tour, so much so that the guide had to use the microphone to be heard.

"May I have your attention for a few moments, please?" He waited briefly for the passengers on the tour bus to quiet down before speaking again. "Well, I hope you enjoyed Roatan's not so best kept secret...a little piece of paradise, would you say? We have three more stops to make. Our first stop is a shopping plaza where you can buy souvenirs. Then we'll stop at the chocolate factory for a brief lesson on the process of chocolate making. I'm assuming you all like chocolate?"

The group answered without hesitation with a collective and very loud, "Yes!"

"Good. Our last stop is the rum cake shop... and don't worry...if you don't drink rum...you can eat it!"

We all had a good laugh. Peter looked at me and said, "Chocolate and rum cake? My god, can this day get any better?"

I looked into his piercing blue eyes, "Thank you for this wonderful day, Peter." I held his arm tightly and leaned my head on his shoulder.

"And the day just got better," he whispered into my ear.

Our tour bus reached the resort in the early evening. We got off the bus, and Peter and I stood aside waiting for our new friends on the circular driveway.

"It has been a pleasure spending the day with you," said the lady with the floppy hat.

"The pleasure is all ours," I replied.

"Let's meet up for drinks before the end of the week. We'll see you around for sure. Have a great evening!" said Peter to the couple before yelling at me. "See you in the room, hon!" as he took off in a flash.

"My God, my God, he must be in some sort of hurry," the lady with the floppy hat said.

"Washroom break," I said laughing. I made an excuse for Peter, and she gave me a knowing smile.

"Do you mind if I give you my number, so you can send me those pictures? Once my phone is charged, I'll reply, so we can plan a time for drinks together and look over the pictures."

"Absolutely," she said as she pulled out her phone.

"She never goes anywhere without her phone," her husband teased.

The lady with the floppy hat gave her husband a look of disapproval.

"Sorry, but we never introduced ourselves properly. I'm Jen, and my husband who can't stop mocking me is Ben."

"I'm Misty, and my boyfriend's name is Peter. And once again, thank you very much for taking those pictures for us. Hope to see you guys later. Enjoy your evening."

"You, too!" Jen and Ben said in unison as we parted ways.

Roatan, the island where memories are made.

CHAPTER 8

*Stress, like darkness, will not last when
happiness and light enter your soul.*

I was dying for a drink and a shower while
feeling a little light headed at the same
time. *Was it the heat? Or maybe the rum cake?*

"Hi, hon!" I called out to Peter as I entered
the room. Peter did not answer. I could hear the
water running in the shower. I grabbed a bottle
of cold water from the fridge and drank it as fast
as I could. And then...

"Sweetheart! Misty! Wake up! Can you hear
me?"

I found myself lying on the floor of the room
with Peter standing over me.

"Misty, please talk to me. Are you okay?" He implored.

"I'm okay, I think. What happened?"

"I came out of the washroom and found you lying down on the floor. You must have passed out. Are you sure you're alright?"

"I think so," I said as I slowly sat up. "I was feeling very thirsty, and I downed a bottle of cold water from the fridge. I don't remember anything after that."

"Maybe the cold water was a shock to your system? You must be more careful."

"It's strange, Peter, this has never happened to me before."

I tried to get up, but my head was still spinning. My body felt like a heavy weight was holding me down. The walls were whirling around me. I closed my eyes and felt awful—dizzy, woozy, unsteady.

"Why don't you lie down for a bit, and I'll get you a bottle of water that has not been refrigerated and some fresh fruit, it will make you feel better," said Peter as he helped me up and walked me to the bed.

"Thanks, hon. Lying down helps. I'm feeling a little better already. I must have had a heat stroke. It's my fault for staying in the sun too long and not drinking enough water."

I laid down, closed my eyes, and tried to relax. It did not take me long to fall asleep and when I woke up, I was a bit restless. Peter was gone, looking for water bottles and fresh fruit to help me gain back my strength. I got up to test myself. I was fine and my first instinct was to check my phone for new messages. I pulled it out from my beach bag and then remembered that the phone had not been charged. *Darn.* Suddenly I began wondering about what could have happened to Julia. *Did Scott check out the fabric under the dock to see if it matched Julia's scarf?*

I hadn't had a single thought about Julia all day long. It didn't seem fair that I had been enjoying a carefree day when she could be in desperate need of help...or worse. But what could I do, really? I wanted so badly to share my concerns with Peter, but I knew there was no point. In fact, he had been very adamant about it, and

I was afraid that he would be furious with me if I brought up the subject again. Sometimes I didn't understand him. Why was he acting that way? All these thoughts made me feel anxious. *There I go again. I can't stop myself from worrying. Peter is right. I must stop, or I'll drive myself crazy.* I sat on the edge of the bed and did some breathing exercises.

In through the nose…out through the mouth… repeat…

I heard the door open. It was Peter returning with fresh water bottles and fruit.

"Hey hon, how are you feeling?"

"Much better. Thanks."

Peter walked over to me and handed me a piece of pineapple. "Eat this, it'll help you get your strength back," he said.

I took a bite to please him. "I could really use a shower, darling. Perhaps if I feel better after we could go for a nice walk along the beach before dinner."

"Good idea. Go have your shower, but please keep the door open, just in case."

"You're so sweet, Peter, but believe me, I'm fine. Really."

Peter kept a close watch on me as I made my way to the bathroom. I thought about how nice it was to have someone to take care of me. I always prided myself on being independent, especially after my breakup with my previous boyfriend, Seth. I had been sort of happy on my own for a long time. But then I met Peter, and he made me feel special. All was going well between us until he started bossing me around. It must stop. *I have to tell him this can't go on, otherwise there'll be no future for us.*

I took a long hot shower. It worked its magic on my body and spirit. I did some more deep breathing exercises and took my time enjoying the feeling of warm water running down my body. After my shower I applied fresh makeup, slipped into a cocktail dress, and announced to Peter that I was ready for our walk before dinner.

"Wow!" exclaimed Peter in his deep voice, and then he muttered something under his breath.

I didn't understand what he had said. And frankly, I was a bit surprised by the tone of his voice. I thought he was reacting to some breaking news on the TV, which was blaring.

"What did you say? I can barely hear you. Please turn off the TV."

"You look HOT!"

I was flattered. It had been a while since Peter had complimented me. It felt good.

"Why don't we forget about dinner and go straight to dessert." He walked over to me, wrapped his arms around my waist, and gave me a full-blown deep kiss on the mouth. His tongue was searching for more, and I reacted in kind.

I needed to breathe and let go of him. "Easy, stud. Let's go for a short walk first."

"I'll hold you to this promise," he sighed and pretended to pout.

"I really need some fresh air and some food to regain my strength, Peter. I'll feel much better after that."

"I understand, sweetheart." He held onto my hand as we walked out the room.

"How about a walk outside of the resort for a change of scenery? I noticed a little plaza down the road when we were on the tour bus."

Peter liked the idea and led the way as we strolled along the main road. It was a five-minute walk to the plaza. We browsed through a few souvenir shops, and I could tell Peter was getting bored. I took his hand and led him outside.

"Let's head down this laneway towards the beach and then back to the bar on the resort for cold drinks."

"That's the best idea you've had all day," he replied, thankful that the shopping excursion was over.

We reached the beach where the laneway ended and stopped to orient ourselves. Peter looked lost and kept looking around. I let him wander around for a while before pointing my finger to the right. It had not taken me long to recognize where we were. Vintage Pearl, where we had celebrated my birthday, was just ahead of us. Peter wrapped his arm around my shoulder as we passed by. We kept on walking and soon made it to the docks where the water taxis and the glass bottom boat were moored. The memory of the piece of cloth tangled beneath the ocean surface was still troubling me. I pulled away from Peter and walked towards the docks to take a long look at the water taxis.

"What is it, Misty?"

"Nothing. I just want to ask the water taxi fellow over there a few questions. There may be other places on the island we might want to see."

Peter looked at me and then stared at the water taxi driver. "Oh, right, I see. Any excuse to talk to a good-looking guy."

"I hadn't noticed he was so cute." I said with a smirk. "Thanks for pointing it out to me, hon. I won't be long."

As I made my way to the dock, I recognized the water taxi driver as the same fellow that I had seen after our glass bottom boat tour. The young taxi driver used the same cheesy line as before when he saw me walking in his direction.

"This is *The Love Boat*! Please come aboard, I was expecting you!"

I gave him a friendly smile, thinking that he'd better change his line if he wanted to be more successful.

"Hi, I was thinking of going for a boat ride, and I was just wondering, where do you usually take your passengers?"

"I can take you anywhere, but most people like me to take them to Little French Key."

"Oh? We were just there! It is an amazing place!"

"I can take you there right now or tomorrow if you'd prefer."

"Thank you. I think I'll ask my boyfriend first if he wants to go there again."

"Boyfriend? No boyfriends allowed on my boat. I'll take you to the best beach on the island and show you a good time."

"Oh!" I blurted out, unsure what to say. He laughed, thinking that he had scored a good line. I felt a little awkward and grinned shyly, "I don't think my boyfriend would approve, but thank you for the offer." I left quickly and walked back to where Peter was waiting. I could see that he was not happy.

"What did you ask him?"

"As I told you earlier, I wanted to know where he could take us with his water taxi, in case we would like to do some more sightseeing."

"I wouldn't get on a boat with that guy," said Peter with a sour face.

"What? Why?" I couldn't resist teasing him.

"Well, from where I was standing, I could clearly see that he was flirting with you. And when you walked away, he was totally checking you out. He's got one thing on his mind. I wonder how many girls he's taken advantage of."

"Really? You could figure out all that from way over here?" I kept teasing him.

"Do you actually trust that guy?"

Judging by his tone, I could sense that Peter was getting upset.

"Seriously, Misty, you can't trust everyone you meet. I know you always look for the good in people, but sometimes you're so naive. It's going to get you into trouble one of these days."

I chose not to respond. Peter was showing me a side of him that I had not seen before. He could not only be overly protective at times; he also possessed a slight streak of jealousy. *On second thought, he might be right about the water taxi driver. But I prefer to think that he loves me, enough to be so protective.*

I held onto Peter's hand, and we walked in silence until we reached the beach bar. Our friends from the tour were already seated on barstools, waving at us when they saw us. Peter spotted them and walked up to them.

"Hello, hello, folks. Nice to see you again."

Peter sat next to Ben and ordered a beer right away. I grabbed the empty stool next to Jen.

"Hey, how did you like the tour?" I asked Jen.

"It was fantastic. I enjoyed the rum cake so much. I think I'll go back to get some more for the rest of our stay. I know that Ben really enjoyed the tour and that makes me really happy. I must admit though that I felt a bit tired and overheated when we got back to our room, but I jumped in the shower and cooled off quickly. How 'bout you?"

"Same here. But I was also pretty dehydrated. I think I downed a bottle of cold water too fast, and I passed out and fell on the floor."

"Oh my God, are you okay? Did you injure yourself?"

"I'm fine, thanks for asking. Peter took good care of me. He's such a sweetheart."

Peter was sitting across from me, too engrossed in his own conversation with Ben to notice that I was complimenting him.

"Thank God you're alright," Jen said before taking a sip of her drink. "By the way, did you receive the pictures I texted you?"

"I haven't had a chance to check them yet. My phone is still plugged in. Actually, you know what, Jen? It should be fully charged by now. Don't mind me if I run back to my room and get my phone. I would like to take some pictures of the fire show tonight."

"Sure, then we can check to see if you can view the pictures I sent."

The room was literally only a two-minute walk, but somehow, I felt a sense of urgency and started running. As soon as I entered the room, I rushed to the nightstand and grabbed my phone. I had one new text message. It was from Scott.

"I checked out the scarf under the water at the dock. It is a perfect match of the one Julia was wearing in the picture the night she was last seen..."

My heart began to race, "Oh my God!" I gasped and continued reading the text.

"...I have given the scarf to the police and told them how you found it. I don't know what it means, but thank you for your help. I will let you know if there is any more news. —Scott."

I was right, although I didn't want to be. I wanted to cry for her, fearing the worst. I felt panic setting in, and I fought hard to compose myself. I had to get back to the bar before Peter and our friends started wondering why I was taking so long. I took a moment to check myself in the hallway mirror. *Keep strong and carry on*, I told myself. This was the same mantra I repeated to myself often after my father passed away when I was young. It helped me cope with the pain then, and now, whenever I was under stress.

If I add one more worry to my long list, I'm afraid I will suffer from a brain overload and will need a total reboot to function again.

I quickly stepped out of the room and noticed one of those creepy big-eyed crabs crawling towards my foot. "Get lost, ugly crab!" I screamed. I couldn't believe this was happening to me again. I shook it off my foot and dashed back to the beach bar. I was out of breath when I reached the bar but somehow managed to hide it well. Peter was having a serious discussion about the hockey playoffs with Ben. He likely never noticed my absence. Jen smiled when I arrived. I didn't smile back, and she noticed.

"Hey, is everything okay? Are you feeling alright?"

"I'm okay…I think. It's just that I received a text message, and I'm not sure what to make of it."

"Whom is it from?"

"It's from Scott, a guy we met here. He got friendly with a girl at this resort a few days ago.

Her name is Julia. They seemed to have really hit it off but..." I hesitated and wondered how much I should tell Jen. After all, I had just met her.

Jen gave me a probing smile. "Let me guess, it's not going well?"

I swallowed a few times before blurting out, "She's gone missing."

"Missing? What exactly do you mean?"

This time, I took a sip of wine before answering. "She was last seen three nights ago and has not been in her room since. She was supposed to meet Scott for lunch on Wednesday but never showed up or left any message. Scott reported this to the local police, and they are investigating."

"My God! How awful!"

"I know. I wish there was something I could do, but..."

Jen furrowed her brows and encouraged me to continue.

"...but Peter doesn't want me involved. He said it's not our business and to leave it to the police and resort security."

I took another, larger sip of wine and peered down at my half-empty glass. Jen said something, but I was no longer paying attention. I must have zoned out because when I didn't answer, she gently placed her hand on my shoulder and said, "What did the text say?"

"What text?"

"You said you received a text from Scott, and you didn't know what to make of it."

"Oh, yes. Scott found a scarf under the dock where the water taxis are anchored. It's a red scarf like the one Julia was wearing the night she was last seen."

Jen squinted her eyes and said, "But, how would he know to check there?"

"I told him. I noticed the scarf snagged on the dock post when Peter and I took a tour on the glass bottom boat a few days ago. The scarf looked familiar. I thought I had seen it before, but I couldn't be sure. Then the police showed me a picture of Julia wearing a scarf. The picture jogged my memory, and I told Scott to check it out."

"Do you think that..." Jen took a deep breath before speaking again. "Do you think that something happened to her?"

My heart palpitated at the thought. "God, I hope not...but I can't help but wonder...given the circumstances."

"Hey, ladies!" Ben interrupted. "Why do you two seem so serious?"

I looked at Jen and shook my head ever so slightly to make sure that no one else would notice. Jen immediately understood the silent message and nodded her head.

"Let's have some fun, ladies. We're on vacation." Ben draped his arms around our shoulders from behind. Just then the jolly bartender asked if we wanted another drink. Ben answered for us.

"Yes, amigo! Another round for the ladies, please!"

I didn't want another drink. I felt sick with worry for Julia. I wanted to do something, anything other than sitting around and worrying myself to death. But what could I do? Peter was set against any involvement. I could not even mention her name without starting an argument. At least I could talk to Jen. *Thank God for Jen.*

"Jen, I really need to talk to someone about Julia. But please keep it to yourself. Peter would be furious if he knew."

"Sure...of course." Jen put her hand on top of mine and looked me in the eye. "You can trust me." She quietly stared at me for a while and then said, "But why on earth would Peter be furious?"

"I don't understand him sometimes. According to him it's the police's job to find her. Period."

"Well, yeah, it is up to the police, but I think it's totally normal for you to be concerned."

"Thank you for saying that. I can't stop thinking about her, and I'm afraid that she got herself into some kind of trouble. I haven't been able to talk to anyone about it." I looked at Jen with a sense of relief. "But in fairness, there's more to it. Peter also thinks I worry too much about everything under the sun. He made me promise to leave all my worries and stress behind on this vacation. I think he means well. He is trying to protect me. But sometimes..." I hesitated and took another long sip of wine before I continued. "…sometimes I need to talk about what worries me. And when I try to talk to him, he listens for a bit and then he gets angry at me for worrying about matters that he thinks should'nt concern me. I get angry at myself too. I wish I could just let things go, but I just can't. I can't just wish my worries away, if you know what I mean. It just doesn't work that way. And…" I hesitated again and looked towards Peter to make sure he was not able to hear what I was about to confess to Jen.

"And what?" Jen asked,

"I suffer from an anxiety disorder. I've lived with it for years. It's a chronic mental illness. It's more like a curse if you ask me, and there's no cure for it. When I take my medication regularly, I can manage to control my anxiety. I still have my anxious moments but with relaxation techniques, I can deal with daily life stress."

"My dear, there's no shame in that."

"I know, but it's not the worst of it. I forgot to bring my medication on this trip, and I think it's becoming a problem."

"Oh no. Did you try going to a local pharmacy?"

"No, I don't think it's worth the trouble. How would I get there? Peter would find out. Besides, I'll be home in a few days."

Just then, Peter glanced at me, and I caught his questioning look. He was no longer chatting with Ben. Did he sense my uneasiness? He was always so perceptive. I loved that about him, but this time, I didn't want him to pry. As much as it helped to talk to Jen, I was still feeling extremely anxious. I needed a moment to compose myself. I excused myself and headed for the ladies' room. I splashed cold water on my face and stared at myself in the mirror. I faked a full-teeth smile and then laughed at myself. I was feeling a little lightheaded from drinking so much. I wondered if my false smile would fool Peter. I didn't want him to know how I was really feeling. It would provoke questions and inevitably he would find out the truth about my medication.

I walked back to the bar area, carefully watching my steps, not wanting to appear too drunk.

My whole attention was focused on where my feet were landing when a woman zipped past me. I paid no attention to her initially, but when she stopped to look back, I managed to get a quick glimpse of her. I could not believe my eyes. The woman looked so much like Julia. I tried to take a second look at her, but I was too late, she was already gone. I thought for a moment that my eyes were playing tricks on me, or worse, that I was very drunk.

The entire interaction went by in a flash. Was it a mere shadow of someone who reminded me of Julia? But then again, I thought her resemblance to Julia was just too spot-on. I walked away, thoroughly confused. I pulled the barstool to sit down, and I saw Peter from the corner of my eye. He was still chatting about the hockey game with Ben. I didn't think he had noticed me leaving. He surprised me when he suddenly grabbed my hand before I could sit down.

"Hey, hon, where have you been?"

I gave him my best bright phony smile and squeezed his arm. "I just went to the ladies' room."

He seemed satisfied with my answer, so I quickly took my seat next to Jen.

Jen greeted me with a concerned look on her face. "Are you okay, Misty? You look like you've seen a ghost."

I swallowed hard, not knowing how to answer. Finally, I spouted out, "Did you see a girl walk by a minute ago? She had long dark hair, about my age and height."

"No. I've been people watching while you were in the washroom. I didn't notice anyone that fits your description. But you know there are lots of pretty girls on this island."

"I just saw someone who looks just like Julia."

"Are you sure?"

"To tell the truth it happened so fast, I'm not really certain if it was her."

"If it is her, it's great news. But don't you think the police or the resort management would have told you they had found her? I'm sure it was just a girl who happened to look like her."

"You're probably right, but I don't know if I should go back and look for her, just to make sure."

I was confused, stressed, anxious, and drunk. It was overwhelming. I knew that Jen was doing her best to help me. But it was not working, not yet at least. Jen was about to tell me something when Ben stepped behind us and cheerfully said, "Hey, ladies! Can I buy you dinner?"

"It's an old joke, Ben, and it's not funny. So nice of you to invite our friends for dinner when we are in an all-inclusive resort!" Jen winced, not pleased with Ben's interruption, then turned towards me and softly said, "Are you up for dinner with us? Or do you prefer to be alone with Peter?"

"Don't be silly, let's all go to dinner together," I said as I grabbed my purse and phone.

Peter reached for my hand and said, "Is everything okay, sweetheart? We don't have to do dinner right now, if you're not up to it."

"I'm fine, Peter. Let's go together as a group, it'll be fun."

We followed a few steps behind Ben and Jen, who were walking hand in hand like newlyweds. Peter was amused, and he winked at me. I smiled back but inside, I was still wrestling with whether I should tell him about the woman who brushed past me. She did look just like Julia. But truth be told, I was not absolutely certain of what I saw. It happened so fast. It was all a blur really. I kept replaying the moment in my mind over and over to no avail. I cursed myself for not catching up with her and talking to her. *What if I'm imagining things?*

"What were you girls talking about all that time?" Peter asked me.

"Oh, you know…just girl talk, small talk, that sort of thing. What about you guys? Were you talking hockey the whole time?"

"Pretty much," he admitted, and we continued our walk, keeping our more serious inner thoughts to ourselves.

When we reached the main building, I took a quick look around searching for the woman I saw earlier. Ben and Jen were just ahead of us, climbing the stairs, which led to the buffet restaurant. We walked past the gift shop on the way to the stairs. I glanced at the window of the shop and saw a dark-haired girl with her back to me. I instantly let go of Peter's hand and stopped to stare at the woman inside.

"What's wrong, Misty?" He grabbed my arm so hard that I dropped my handbag on the floor. The contents of my bag scattered all over the floor. Peter muttered some sort of an excuse, and we both bent down to gather my things.

"What's with you, Misty? You just stopped walking all of a sudden, for no reason at all."

"I thought I saw Julia in the gift shop."

Peter glanced at the gift shop window. "There's no one in there except for the saleslady. What's the matter with you? Are you imagining things? First the crab, and now this?"

"I did not imagine anything. I saw the crab with my own eyes. And in the gift shop was a girl with dark hair just like Julia... She was there a moment ago, and I saw her."

"Sweetheart, I'm really worried about you. You need to take it easy and stay away from the sun. You had a heatstroke earlier, maybe you are not fully recovered. And by the way, you should not be drinking so much. It does not agree with you. You know that."

Peter took my hand, looked into my eyes, and whispered, in my ear, "Our friends are waiting for us upstairs. Let's have a nice dinner with them and forget all about this."

The hostess welcomed us at the top of the stairs with her all-business smile permanently glued on her face, armed with a spray bottle of hand sanitizer and aiming it at us like a trigger-happy sniper.

"Peter and Misty? Your friends are seated at a table on the terrace. Let me show you the way."

As soon as we were seated, the waitress took our drink order. Peter ordered drinks without consulting me. "A Perrier for the lady and a beer for me."

I smiled politely, but I was annoyed by the way he'd taken charge. Speaking for me was a bad habit Peter had acquired recently. I knew he wanted to show that he was taking care of me, but it bothered me. I could take care of myself, and certainly I could order my own drink. I was not a child, and I hated to be treated that way.

Jen picked up on the vibe and looked at me as if to say *I understand*.

We all got up to help ourselves to the buffet. Peter nudged me at the salad bar and murmured in my ear, "Is something else troubling you?"

"No, I'm fine. Please stop asking me how I feel. I just need to eat a good healthy meal. I'm famished. That is all," I lied, which was something I regretted but found myself doing more and more on this trip.

"Well in that case, let's try to enjoy dinner with our new friends." Peter seemed somewhat taken aback by my abrupt response.

"Deal!" I said as I filled my plate with crab meat and shrimp.

I was the last to return to the table and joined the group mid-conversation. They stopped speaking as soon as I pulled my chair and kept staring at me.

Peter saw my questioning look and immediately tried to fill me in. "Hey sweetheart, Jen was just telling me about their son, Eddy."

"Oh? How old is your son, Jen?" I asked.

"Eddy is twenty-four. Here's a picture of the three of us before we left for Roatan," she said as she displayed a picture on her phone.

"Eddy looks just like Ben." I noticed he was seated in a wheelchair but made no mention of it.

"A very handsome fellow! I bet he has lots of girlfriends," I added.

Jen showed the picture to Peter. He smiled, nodded politely, and said, "What happened to Eddy? Did he have an accident?"

"No. He has multiple sclerosis."

"Oh, I'm sorry to hear that," Peter said.

I glanced at Ben, who had a sad look on his face. Jen, on the other hand, was quick to reply.

"Don't be sorry. He doesn't let it stop him from anything. He landed his first job a year ago.

He's a dispatcher at a taxi company. He saved some money and paid for this vacation as a gift for our twenty-fifth wedding anniversary. That's why we took so many pictures. They're not for us or for Facebook. They're for Eddy."

"What a good son you have! What a beautiful and generous thing to do for his parents. You must be so proud of him," I chimed in when I saw the hurt in Ben's eyes.

We quietly ate our meal and kept the conversation light for the rest of the evening. Peter discussed hockey with Ben, which was always a safe bet with a fellow Canadian. Jen and I complimented the resort and exchanged shopping gift ideas for Eddy. The evening went by quickly, and I remembered going straight to our room after dinner. I must have fallen asleep as soon as my head hit the pillow. There was so much to discuss with Peter. But I was mentally too exhausted.

When will I find the courage to clear the air, once and for all?

CHAPTER 9

In darkness we long for light.
In light we fear darkness.

I got up in the middle of the night to use the washroom. I was wide awake, and all kinds of thoughts were racing through my mind. *Was the girl in the gift shop Julia? Or was my mind playing a trick on me? And what about Scott? We haven't seen him for a while. What's going on with him? I should text him in the morning to see if he has heard anything.*

I wished I could talk to Peter about all of this, but I knew he would tell me that I'm driving myself crazy. I splashed water on my face and glanced at myself in the mirror. I looked old and tired. *I'm a worrier. Peter is right.*

The room was pitch dark. I was careful not to bump into the furniture as I made my way back to bed. The last thing I wanted to do was to wake up Peter. He could be such a grouch if his sleep was disturbed. I pulled the blanket over my body, shut my eyes, and recited a mantra I had used in the past to clear my mind.

Be present.

Be grateful for this moment.

Let go of thoughts that don't serve you.

There is nothing I can do for anyone in this moment except for myself.

I needed to regain my peace of mind and focus on myself. I thought about how lucky I was to be warm and cozy in bed beside someone like Peter who truly cared for me. He was a good man with good intentions but needed to take a hard look at how he was treating me lately. Things between us could be so much better if only he trusted me a little bit more—another worry that at times did more harm than good. I did not want to be ruled by my anxiety disorder. Life was too short for that. And if Peter was less intense about it, I could manage it very well by myself. I've done it my whole life. *I very much care for him and wish he would understand what I truly need.*

I breathed deeply, feeling the warmth of Peter's body lying next to me. I was mindful of how perfectly still and quiet everything around me was. After a while, I became aware that the air conditioner had gone silent. It was getting warm in the room, and I removed the blanket from over me. The dull light from the outside hallway, which constantly filtered through the thin slit at the bottom of the door, had vanished. The room was eerily quiet. Time seemed suspended. For one brief moment I felt as if I had been transported far away to a dark empty world.

Peter started to stir in the bed. All of a sudden, I felt a clawlike sensation touch my shoulder, and it startled me.

"Peter! Wake up!" I screamed.

"What? What's wrong?" he mumbled, still half asleep.

"I think there's a crab in the bed!"

"No, there isn't. Go to sleep." He pulled the covers over his face and went back to sleep.

"But I felt it touch my shoulder! Please check the bed, I won't be able to sleep otherwise. Please..."

"Okay! Turn on the light, I can't see shit!"

"The power is out."

"Where's my phone?" I could hear Peter moving around the room and then he shouted, again, "Shit!"

"What's wrong?"

"I stubbed my toe on the bed frame! Dammit! Where's my phone?"

I carefully got up from the bed and felt my way around the pitch-dark room. I finally found Peter's phone on the window's sill.

"I found it!" I shouted. I touched the screen, and it lit up. Peter grabbed the phone and fumbled with it for a while. He swore some more before he found the flashlight button and turned it on. He then shone the light on me.

"What's with you? I was deep asleep!"

"Sorry, but I don't want to sleep with a crab in my bed, do you?"

"Do you really want me to answer that?"

"Just check the bed!" I realized I was hysterical which was not helping. I lowered my voice to a plea, "Please, Peter."

Peter shone the light on the bed. I stripped the covers and shook them. There were no crabs.

"The only crab here is in your head!" Peter barked.

"Seriously, Peter! Please check the floor and under the bed."

"No crab there, either!"

"But I felt a claw on my shoulder!"

"You must have been dreaming."

"No, I don't think so. Something scratched me. If not a crab, what could it be?"

"I don't know, but there's nothing here. Maybe it was just a bad dream." Peter sat on the bed beside me and tried to calm me down.

"Look sweetheart, I'm sorry that I yelled at you. I overreacted. I know. To tell you the truth, this whole business about Julia has been bothering me as well. I'm troubled by it too. But above all, I am really concerned about the way it has been affecting you. I understand why you are so distressed. You care, and you always want to help others, even if it's at your own expense. But believe me, you can't solve the world's problems on your own. Sometimes you just need to take a break and stop thinking about all the things that could be wrong. Time has a way of fixing things without our intervention."

He stopped talking and patted the bed beside him. He smiled, and I closed my eyes and nodded.

"Let's go back to sleep. Nothing like a good night's rest to chase away our worries. Tomorrow is another day."

There were a lot of truths about what Peter had said. If only I could think like him. Unfortunately, my brain was not programmed that way. Besides, right now I was more confused and embarrassed to be able to think clearly. I closed my eyes, but no matter how hard I tried, I could not fall asleep.

What's wrong with me?
Am I losing it?

CHAPTER 10

"The strongest people are those who win battles we know nothing about."

—Unknown

I woke up later that morning alone in bed. The room was dark. The thick curtains were an effective defense against the bright sunshine beating down on the sleepy resort. I assumed Peter was in the washroom. I felt well-rested despite the incident in the middle of the night. I reached for my phone to check the time. It was nine o'clock. I overslept. I normally get up at seven, an old habit I had acquired from years of getting to work early. *Why didn't Peter wake me?* The bathroom door was ajar, but Peter was not there. I turned on the light and saw a note on the sink.

"Sweetheart, you were sleeping so soundly, I didn't want to disturb you. I went for breakfast, and then I'm having coffee by the pool. Come join me when you're ready. —Peter"

I hated sleeping late on vacation. It felt like taking time away from my holiday. If I needed to rest, I could do so by the pool or on the beach. I was annoyed with myself. I took a long shower and enjoyed the sensation of the hot water flowing on my shoulders and back. I closed my eyes and tried to clear my mind. *I need to do this more often, just be in the moment and stop obsessing about everything...my job, my relationship with Peter, the environment, other people's problems. My sanity depends on it.*

I stepped out of the shower and while toweling myself, I recited the mantra my late father had taught me about the importance of maintaining a positive attitude. Saying it out loud had helped me through many tough times. It made me think of him and his amazing strength of character. He had suffered a devastating stroke at the age of fifty-four. He was bedridden for the last three years of his life, but his mind and spirit were as strong as ever. He fell ill at the same time Christopher Reeve, the actor who played Superman, suffered his near fatal horse-back riding accident. I would tell my father to be strong like Superman, and he would laugh at me. My father was my hero. *If only I could be as strong as him.*

Before his stroke, my father lived a rich life, not in extravagance but in the riches of family and education. He was many things, a civic leader, a teacher, an entrepreneur, a passionate traveler with an open-mind and genuine curiosity for diversity. He dedicated his entire life to the well-being of his family and community. He and my mother taught me to appreciate the unique-ness of each individual. "Treat others as you wish to be treated. Don't be quick to judge."

My father came from humble beginnings, my grandparents were new immigrants from

Poland. Life back then was hard, my father always reminded us. But somehow, they managed, he often proudly told us.

He met my mother, his future wife, at a Polish wedding. Although the love was always there, like any marriage there were bumps along the road. My mother was bipolar. Her ups and downs could be a roller coaster of a ride for our family. "*It's not her fault. She just needs to take her medication. Just like I take mine for my blood pressure.*" He would tell me and my sister, in moments of crises. And when my mother's lows were particularly severe, and I could not stop crying, he would take me in his arms. *It's not her fault. She will get better. Be positive. Be patient…*

He took care of mom, the best way he knew how. Then after his stroke mom nursed him. And when my father passed away, my sister and I looked after my mom, when her mind took her to dark places.

Unconditional love.

I walked out of the bathroom in good spirits. I felt rejuvenated by the fond memory of my father. Something came over me and I started singing an old favorite of mine, "I Am Woman," while getting dressed.

I slipped on a floral sundress, attempted to fix my out-of-control frizzy hair and headed out towards the main building. I was looking forward to spending another beautiful day at the resort with Peter. I spotted him lounging by the pool area. I called out his name, but he did not respond. He was sitting at a table, engrossed with something he was reading on his cell phone. *More of the same. Why expect him to change?* I approached him and gently tapped his shoulder. It startled him.

"Sorry Peter, I didn't mean to scare you."

"Oh, hey, sweetie, it's okay, I was just catching up on some news and emails." He quickly put his phone down.

"Sorry about all the excitement last night."

"Don't worry about it. Hey, do you mind eating by yourself? I already ate, and I need to reply to a few emails. Work, sorry." He made a face, no doubt remembering how he'd admonished me last night.

"No, I don't mind. I brought my book and would like to enjoy it while having my breakfast."

"Okay sweetheart, enjoy yourself and come back here when you finish." He leaned over to give me a peck on the cheek. I felt reassured that all was well again between us.

I took my time walking back to the main building, admiring the beautifully manicured grounds, smelling the salt in the air, and for the first time noticing how happy everyone was on the resort. When I reached the top of the stairs, I stopped for a moment to enjoy the magnificent ocean view one more time. *There is so much beauty here. I don't want to ever forget this sight.*

The restaurant was packed that morning with the fresh arrival of vacationers. They all seemed in a hurry to fill their already overflowing plates as much as possible, fearing perhaps that the resort would run out of food. I managed to grab a table in the shaded corner of the terrace. Leaving behind my beach bag to ensure that no one would take my place, I headed for the buffet bar with wide, hungry eyes. I ordered a veggie omelet and waited patiently for the cook to prepare it. That's when I noticed Scott sitting alone in the other far end corner inside the dining room. He was not eating and kept looking around, as if he was expecting someone.

I was tempted to join him but then thought I might be intruding. After another quick glance in his direction, I finally made up my mind to return to my table. I sat for another minute or two, pondering some more about what to do about Scott. I ate a few bites of my breakfast and downed a half cup of coffee. Then I thought about my resolution earlier in the morning: *I am strong. I am invincible.* I took a deep breath, and headed inside the restaurant to look for Scott.

Scott looked tanned and healthy. Roatan had done good work on his physical appearance. But he seemed a bit tense for someone on vacation. I stood in front of him but he didn't notice me. He was focused on a text message he was reading on his iPhone.

"Hey, you!" I said, waiting for him to tear away his eyes from his phone.

He looked up at me, took his time to refocus, and after a few long seconds finally acknowledged me. "Oh, hey Misty, how are you?"

He didn't wait for my response and immediately turned his attention back to his phone, leaving me standing in front of him like a fool. Somewhat flustered, I decided to confront him with a question that would certainly spark his interest.

"Have you heard anything about Julia?"

Once again, he took his time answering me. "Not really. All I know is that the police are asking around to see if anyone has seen her."

"Scott, maybe I could be of some help. Maybe I could show her picture around?"

"No!" Scott shouted. "Don't do that! Leave it to the police. It's their job. It's not your business."

He sounded just like Peter. As a matter of fact, he had used Peter's exact words. It irritated me greatly. This was the first time I experienced his bad temper. I now recalled what Officer Juan had told me about him. I was more than upset. I was offended by the way he'd spoken to me and even more to the point, angry at Peter for talking to Scott behind my back. *Peter will hear from me.* But for now, I needed to get something from Scott, and I was not about to be deterred by his bad manner. I swallowed my pride and continued pressing Scott.

"But Scott, I don't understand why you don't want my help. The more people help, the better chance we have of finding her." I spoke in a tone that would not allow any counterargument. I was determined to go ahead with my plans to help find Julia.

Scott stared at me, seemingly looking for an appropriate response. He was definitely taken aback by my assertiveness. He looked around the room to see if anyone was within earshot who might overhear our conversation. He finally made up his mind that a tactical retreat was his best way out.

"Misty, I have to go, please excuse me." Scott stood up, but I remained standing in his way. I had more to say, and I wasn't going to budge.

"Scott, I was the one who found the scarf, remember?"

"Yes."

"Then maybe there's more I can do."

"Then talk to the police, not me," he replied as he nudged me aside and started to walk away.

"I saw someone yesterday who looked just like Julia!" I shouted as he turned his back to me.

It had the desired effect on him. Scott stopped in his tracks and stared at me sideways. "What are you talking about?" It sounded more like a dare than a question.

I raised the stakes one more notch and challenged him to prove me wrong. "I saw Julia in the gift shop last night."

"That's impossible." I could see the indecision in his face. He was clearly shaken.

"Why is that impossible?"

"Because the police or the resort security would have told me if they had found her or that she was back at the resort."

"Maybe they didn't get around in telling you, Scott. But I know what I saw in the gift shop. Peter was with me."

"So, what did Peter say? And why didn't you ask her where she has been?"

"We got distracted when I dropped my purse, and everything fell out. Peter bent down to help me. When we looked up again in the gift shop, she was gone."

Scott recovered quickly from his initial shock. "Well in that case we'll eventually catch up with her. Won't we? But you know what I think, Misty? I don't doubt you saw someone in the gift shop. But it was not Julia. It was probably just someone you thought looked like her."

"I guess that's possible. But unless you help me look for her, we will never know, won't we?" I said daring him again to challenge me.

Scott did not answer right away. He brushed away his long red hair while surveying the room. He was obviously stalling once again. Seemingly running out of options, he finally looked at me and sheepishly said, "Look, sorry, Misty, I really have to go. I'll talk to you later."

Scott rushed off leaving me behind feeling very frustrated that I had not been able to convince him to let me help him find Julia.

What's going on? First Peter, now Scott doubting me. Am I obsessing about nothing, as Peter said?

"Pardon me, miss." I turned around to see a waitress trying to get my attention.

"Yes, what is it?"

"Do you want to move to this table? I can bring your plate over if you want."

"No, thank you. I was speaking to someone who just left."

She seemed confused. Scott was long gone, and I was not sure if she believed me.

"I'll go back to my table, thank you."

I wasn't feeling hungry anymore. I took a few bites of the omelet, which was cold by now, and drank what was left of the orange juice. I then stood up still fuming and headed straight for the gift shop. Inside there was a new salesgirl, who was busy folding T-shirts. Before the salesgirl had a chance to make her sales pitch, I asked her about the girl who worked last night. Unfortunately, I was informed that she was off for the remainder of the week. *No luck there either.*

I left the main building and stood outside staring at the ocean with frustration brewing inside of me for the longest time. I thought about Peter and Scott's aggressive attitude towards me and wondered if there was something they were not telling me. It was unnerving to say the least. I closed my eyes, raised my head straight up facing the sky, and let the sun's rays warm my face and soothe my nerves. It did not help. There was only one thing clear to me. Peter and Scott were wrong. We could not count on the local police alone. After all, I was the one who had found Julia's scarf.

I began walking again, not caring very much where I was going. I strolled slowly along the winding path, stopping to admire the blooms on the manicured shrubs, doing everything possible to ease my angst. I finally reached the pool area, where I saw Peter chatting with someone. From where I was standing, I could not precisely tell who it was, as a palm tree was partially obstructing my view. A glimpse of the curly mop of red hair confirmed my suspicion. Scott and Peter seemed to be having a heated discussion. I could not make out what they were arguing about except for a few snippets here and there spoken louder…defensive…unrelenting…weird. All of sudden, Scott looked in my direction and abruptly ended his conversation with Peter and left before I arrived.

"Hey, sweetheart," said Peter when he saw me.

He looked at me with an odd expression. I could not figure out if he was happy to see me. Not that it mattered, because what I wanted to tell him could not wait.

"I saw Scott talking to you, but he seemed to want to rush off when he saw me coming. What's going on?" My tone was clear enough. I wanted an honest answer to that question.

"Oh, nothing much. We were just talking about the hockey game."

"Hockey! Really, Peter, you can do better than that."

Peter exhaled and looked away from me. The long silence that ensued was unbearable. But I stood my ground, determined to get the truth out of him. After a while, Peter gave a long sigh. And I knew then that I'd get my answer.

"Scott's a bit worried about you."

"Me? Why?"

"I knew this was going to upset you. I shouldn't have mentioned it."

"I'm fine! I just wish to help find a girl who is missing! What's wrong with that? What's wrong with expressing my concern over a fellow human being?"

"Calm down, Misty. You're making a scene. Don't you see how stressed out you're getting? We're supposed to be on vacation for God's sake! So, let's try to enjoy ourselves a little bit and let the police handle this...please, sweetheart."

"I see. A girl travelling alone has vanished on a remote island, at the far end of the world, but we should not worry about her. You and Scott are on the same page, right! Let's enjoy ourselves and forget that a girl Scott dated has gone missing."

"He only had one dinner date with her, Misty. So, let's not dramatize things. Besides, what do you know about Julia?"

"Not much, other than that she seemed to be a nice girl, she came alone to this resort, and that your buddy, yes, your good buddy Scott, has the hots for her. Since we're on the subject, tell me how well you know Scott?"

"What about Scott?"

"Well for one thing, he made her cry that day on the beach. What did he do or say to get her so upset? Do you know, Peter? And what about the way their dinner date ended? She cut the date short, and slammed the door in his face, remember!"

"What are you getting at, Misty?"

"I don't know, Peter. You're the smart one. You figure it out. Right now, I feel like going for a swim!" I shouted and stormed off.

I went back to our room, grabbed a towel, rolled it and placed it in my beach bag. My iPhone was on the counter, and I deliberated briefly if I should take it with me. The last thing I needed right now was any more bad news. But the fear of missing out on something important concerning Julia was too much for me to bear, so I took my phone, threw it in the bag, and headed for the pool.

I tossed my things on the lounge chair beside Peter. He looked up at me, but I looked away. I jumped into the pool and swam...and swam... I must have done at least twenty laps. I only slowed down to avoid other bathers. At one point, I overheard a young boy say to his mother, "Wow, look how fast she swims!" It felt good. Out of breath, I raised my body out of the water at the edge of the infinity pool. I looked out at the ocean, which stretched far into the horizon. And then I began to think...*What if... what if Julia felt like I was feeling right now? What if she just wanted to get away from everything and everyone? It would explain why she came to Roatan alone. It would certainly explain why she kept on losing her phone. But she seemed so*

*vulnerable, here in Roatan all by herself. What if
someone had taken advantage of her?*

So many thoughts. So many questions. So
few answers.

I turned to see what Peter was doing by the
pool. It really bothered me that Peter and Scott
were talking about me behind my back. I dove
into the water and swam fast again. I lost count
of how many laps I'd done. It didn't matter. It
was a mindless exercise meant to clear my mind.
When I stepped out of the pool, I noticed Peter
watching me intensely. He hadn't moved a single inch from his chair.

"That was quite a powerful swim."

"Yes. It felt really good, but I still need to go
for a walk. Do you mind?"

Peter said nothing. His expression clearly
answered the question. He had seen me in this
state before and knew better than to argue with
me. I put on my beach wrap, slipped on my
flip-flops, and headed for the warm sand of the
beach. At the edge of the water where the tide
was slowly receding, I removed my flip-flops

and allowed my feet to sink into the wet sand. I listened to the sound of the waves making their slow retreat away from the shores to the open sea. High above me, the sun was making its perpetual shift across the horizon, sending its warm rays on my face like a reminder that better days were to come.

My walk along the beach shore subconsciously led me to the docks where the water taxis were anchored. A woman was standing on the edge of the dock, looking down into the water. Her dark hair was flowing with the ocean breeze. She stood there, alone, staring down at the murky water for a long time. Then she raised her head and looked out into the vast ocean, like someone searching for an answer. All of a sudden, she turned around and started walking in my direction. The water taxi drivers were waving at her, attempting to get her attention, but she ignored them. I took a few steps, feeling compelled to meet her halfway. She looked so familiar. We finally met at the edge of the dock. And there she was. The woman I'd been looking for!

"Julia?" I gasped and put my hand on my mouth.

She stared at me for a very long time. She had beautiful eyes, which seemed to be questioning me more than simply observing me.

"Who are you?" she curtly said.

"Misty. I'm Misty. We met at the resort. Don't you remember me? Where have you been? Are you okay? I've been so worried about you. Have you seen Scott?"

"Who is Scott?"

I was perplexed. I had no doubt in my mind that this was Julia.

In the soft voice of a shy person, she said, "I'm not Julia."

"Oh? I'm so sorry! It's just that you look and even sound so much like..."

"Like Julia," she cut me off. "I'm her twin sister."

"Oh my God!" I blurted. I was left speechless.

"I'm Cheryl. How do you know my sister?"

"I met her at the resort a few days ago. Do you know where she is?"

Cheryl took a deep breath before answering me, "No." And all of a sudden, she started to cry uncontrollably. I didn't know what to do, so I did the only thing that came to my mind. I hugged her and gently rubbed her back.

It was my turn to cry. My eyes went blurry as I tried to console Julia's sister. I released her from my arms and wiped my eyes. I took her hand and slowly led her to two nearby chairs. We sat down, and I waited for her to speak while still trying to make sense of the fact that Julia had an identical twin sister.

"I got a call from the Roatan police saying Julia was missing from the resort. I took the first flight out to Roatan from Toronto. I've been looking for her since I arrived."

I sighed heavily. "So have we. But we have had no luck either."

She kept sobbing. "The police assured me that they're doing everything they can to find her. But so far, they have no idea where she could be."

"Don't worry, it's a small island, I'm sure they will find her. Where are you staying?"

She brushed her hair back behind her ears, like I'd seen Julia do often. "Infinity Bay."

I smiled at the answer, feeling somewhat relieved. "Oh, that's where I must have seen you. Were you at the gift shop last night?"

"Yeah, I guess so. I was feeling my way around the resort."

"I could have sworn I saw Julia at the gift shop, but now I know it was you!" I couldn't wait to tell Peter that I was not imagining things. *He owes me a big apology.*

"You said you met Julia. Did she tell you anything about what her plans were?"

"Not really. All I know is that she met this guy, Scott, had one dinner date with him, and the next day she went missing. But exactly what did the police tell you they were doing to find your sister?"

"Not much. They told me that they interviewed the staff, checked other resorts in case she decided to switch places. They also promised me that they'll let me know as soon as they have any news."

"Did they tell you if they interviewed the crew of the glass bottom boat?"

"No. They did not make any mention of that."

"What about the water taxi drivers? Surely, they must have talked to them?"

"Sorry, Misty, I've no clue what the police have done to find my sister, other than what I've told you."

An idea suddenly popped into my mind.

"Cheryl, would you excuse me for a moment. I'll be right back."

I walked over to the docks, leaving behind a very puzzled looking Cheryl. I was looking for the handsome taxi driver who called himself The Love Boat Captain. An older man was staring at me with a rope in his hand. He looked friendly enough, so I decided to speak to him first.

"Excuse me," I said to the old man.

"Where can I take you, miss?"

"Nowhere, sorry. I just have a question."

"No, I'm not married. Would you like a date with me?" And he burst out laughing. He was missing most of his front teeth, and I couldn't help but smile back.

"I was wondering if you know the driver who calls himself *The Love Boat Captain*?"

He took a deep breath and sighed. "Yes of course. The young ladies always prefer a ride with The Love Boat Captain. I understand," he said, pretending to pout.

"Oh, no, I'm not looking for a taxi ride with him. I just need to ask him a question. I may have left something on his boat. Do you know where I can find him?"

"He's taken the morning off, and he normally shows up for work after lunch late in the afternoon. You can check back later on today. I'll tell him a pretty girl is looking for him when I see him."

"That'll be great. Thank you, sir."

Cheryl gave me a questioning look when I returned.

"What was that all about?"

"There's a young taxi driver who keeps an eye on all the beautiful women on the island. I was just wondering if he had seen Julia by any chance. He's off now, but he's expected back this afternoon. I'll check with him later on."

"Do you really think he would know something?"

"I don't know. Worth a try, I guess."

Cheryl did not seem too convinced but went along. "So, what's next?"

"Let's head back to the resort. Maybe we can get an update from the police… and then maybe we can grab some lunch. I'll introduce you to Scott if you want."

"Okay," Cheryl said softly as she stood up waiting for me to guide her.

During our short walk back to the resort, I took the opportunity to tell Cheryl everything I knew about Julia. I mentioned how Julia met Scott and how Scott thought they had hit it off and had dinner the night she was last seen. I mentioned that Scott went to check on her the next morning, but he could not find her and apparently, she hadn't slept in her room that night. Then I told her about Julia not showing up for her lunch date with Scott the next day. I also told her about Scott alerting resort security and the police questioning Peter and myself. Then I told her a bit about myself and mentioned that I was on vacation with Peter.

When we finally made it to the pool area, I caught sight of Peter and Scott sitting together at a table under an umbrella, each holding a bottle of beer. As we got closer, Peter made eye contact with me. Then he squinted his eyes and nudged Scott with his elbow. They both stared at Cheryl, as if they had seen an apparition. They stood up at the same time and rushed to meet us halfway.

"Jul…" Scott began to speak and then choked on his word. He studied Cheryl's face not believing his eyes. Looking happy, he turned to look at me, searching for some form of confirmation. Then turned his attention to Peter, who was watching Scott's reaction.

"This is Cheryl, Julia's sister," I said, feeling sorry that I was disappointing Scott.

"What? Really?" Scott's expression turned from joyful to utter amazement.

"So you're the fellow who is dating my sister?" she paused to size up Scott. "I arrived in Roatan yesterday when I heard that Julia had gone missing from the resort."

Peter found his voice, "Wow, this is a surprise. You look so much like Julia."

"Thank you, Peter, for the compliment. Julia is my twin sister."

"Have you found your sister?"

"Sadly, not yet, Peter. I'm here looking for her, and I'm really concerned that no one seems to know where she is."

"Did you check with the local police? Did they tell you anything?"

"Not really. They told me that they are looking for her, but they still don't have any clues of her whereabouts."

"But surely, they must have some leads by now. It's been, what, two days since she disappeared?" said Peter.

It should not have come as a huge surprise to learn that Julia had a twin sister. After all, we knew so little about her background. The closest to her had been Scott. He had spent the most time with her and yet he seemed even more shocked than Peter and I, when Cheryl appeared before us. The resemblance was striking. I observed Scott as he was eyeing Cheryl. He looked ill at ease, at a loss for words. Not believing his eyes, the poor fellow must have felt like he was having a flashback. I empathized with Scott and felt compelled more than ever to find Julia. But what came next was a total shock to all of us.

Out of nowhere, Scott blabbered, "I'm sorry for your loss."

I looked at Scott with wide angry eyes, irritated by his insensitivity. *What a dumb thing to say.*

Realizing his mistake, Scott tried to hastily take back what he had said. "Sorry, I didn't mean anything by that. It was wrong of me. I can't imagine what you are going through. You must be so worried."

I was so disappointed with Scott. Although he was obviously trying to make amends, it was just not working.

"Yes, I'm worried sick. It's just not like her to disappear like that. I just pray that she is safe and unharmed." Cheryl tried to fight a tear and quickly looked away.

We just stood staring at her feeling helpless not knowing what to say. After much hesitation, I pulled Cheryl to the side and told her that we had better go to lunch. It was just an excuse to get away from Peter and Scott. I could sense that she needed some space, and besides, I was anxious to talk to the police and to have a brief chat with the water taxi driver who was due back soon.

Peter and Scott exchanged looks, trying to figure out what to do next.

Peter filled in the silence. "Misty, can I speak to you for a moment?" Peter motioned for me to come closer.

"Yes, Peter. What is it?"

"I thought we were having lunch together?"

"You're welcome to join us if you want."

"I think you should give Cheryl some time to herself." Peter was not always that tactful. And this time I knew that he was choosing his words carefully. Perhaps our quarrel earlier had had some beneficial effect on him after all.

"What you really mean is that I shouldn't get involved."

Peter sighed but kept his cool. "I really want to have lunch with you here at the beachside cafe. That's all."

I rolled my eyes and sighed. "Alright, but first, you owe me an apology."

"You are right. I apologize for doubting you."

"What about?"

"Come on, Misty, you know why. I should not have doubted you when you told me last night that you saw someone who looked like Julia. I'll never do that again. I promise."

"And what else?'

"What do you mean?"

"What about the crabs?"

"But I never saw the crabs, Misty."

"But I did. And you did not see Julia's sister in the gift shop, either. But yet you now say you believe me. Do you think I imagine things, Peter?"

"No, of course not. You're right. I should always give you the benefit of the doubt. I'm a fool not to believe you. I'm truly sorry."

I decided to be direct. "That will do for now. You really need to trust me more. You and I need to have a serious conversation. But that's for another time. Meanwhile, let's tell Cheryl and Scott we won't be joining them for lunch."

Cheryl and Scott were chatting while waiting for us. Actually, Cheryl was doing most of the listening, while Scott was babbling away. Her sideways glance at me was a telltale sign that she needed me to come to her rescue.

"Sorry, Cheryl. I promised Peter a lunch date, just for the two of us. Feel free to join us later if you want company. You'll find us here at the pool or at the beach bar."

"Thank you, Misty. I think I'll go back to my room for now. Sorry, Scott, we'll chat some other time perhaps."

The three of us stood like statues in the sand, staring at Cheryl as she walked away. It was quite an eventful day, full of surprises for sure. The shock of finding out that Julia had an identical twin sister had somewhat rescinded in our minds. But I was still left with the awful feeling that something bad might have happened to Julia.

Julia, where are you?

CHAPTER 11

*The mind is a powerful instrument that
sometimes needs guidance.*

"I can't believe how much she looks like Julia. I mean, I know they're twins, but even their mannerisms are the same," said Scott.

Peter and I nodded in agreement. Scott had accompanied us to the resort's only watering hole where Peter and I had found a table at the far end of the bar. It was close enough to the beach to feel the cool ocean breeze—a perfect spot for drinks with Scott before our tête-à-tête lunch. We were about to grab our seats when Scott excused himself.

"Guys, I'll let you eat alone. I'm going for a dive." *What prompted this sudden change?*

Peter was quick to answer, "Okay buddy, hang in there, see you later."

Something was wrong with Scott. He seemed edgy since our encounter with Cheryl. I was certain that his abrupt change of mind was not just an excuse to get away. *What was he really thinking about?* Peter put his hand on my lap sensing that I was not entirely present.

"Hon? Hey, hon?"

I didn't answer.

"Misty!" He said, raising his voice.

"What?"

"Where are you, Misty?"

"I'm here with you. What do you think!"

"Why do you sound upset, then?"

"What would make me upset, Peter?"

"I don't know, Misty. I don't understand you sometimes. And you are doing that thing again."

"What thing?"

"That thing, when you keep staring into space and ignoring me."

My answer was prompt. "I'm not ignoring you, Peter. Can't I have a quiet moment to myself?"

"It's just that you seem…" Peter wavered, not sure if he wanted to complete his sentence. I waited for a second or two and when I was convinced that he was not about to finish, I tried forcing it out of him. I knew where this conversation was heading, and I wanted to get it over with.

"Spell it out, Peter, say what you mean!"

Peter felt the dare in my tone, and this time, he did not hesitate to accept the challenge. "Well, since you asked for it, let me tell you what's on my mind. You seem anxious. You're snippy with me, and you're not paying attention to me. We're on vacation together, but you don't seem to want to be here with me. What's wrong? Is it me? Are you unhappy with me? Maybe you've forgotten to take your medication? Is that it?"

There goes the blame game. Blame the meds when nothing else works. How could I answer that? I didn't want him to know I'd forgotten to bring my anti-anxiety medication with me, for fear of his reaction. Even if that was not the reason why I was so perturbed.

"I'm fine, Peter," I finally said, knowing that my answer would not put an end to our quarrel. Peter always pushed me for more, not that he was argumentative, I felt that he always wanted to have the last word. And therefore, I was expecting a strong retort from him. However, the pain I saw on his face was not something I saw coming. I did not want to hurt him. I just wanted him to be gentle with me. On the other hand, there was a potential element of incompatibility between us that needed to be addressed. I just hoped that it was not irreparable.

Peter kept staring at me with his sad puppy blue eyes. What was I to do? He desired some form of reassurance and I felt the need to give it to him.

"I'm sorry, Peter. I think I'm just really drained and hungry. It makes me grouchy as you well know. Everything is fine between us.

Believe me. And you're totally right, we are wasting precious time. As of now we should make sure to enjoy ourselves." I made excuses. It was easier than admitting the truth. There will be time after this trip to clarify and hopefully remedy our differences.

Just then the waitress came to our table and poured two glasses of cold lemon water. I quickly grabbed my glass and gulped the refreshing water, hoping Peter would do the same.

"May I take your orders?" The waitress asked.

Peter took a deep breath and said, "A burger and salad for me."

Thank God, I sighed in relief. Peter was not dwelling on my meds anymore. "A burger and fries for me."

"Misty, you never order fries! That must be a first."

"I'm on vacation and I want to treat myself." The truth was, I was hungry for comfort food. I desperately needed a quick fix to make me feel better. I had not given up on my intentions to help find Julia. At least not yet. And that made me nervous because I was holding back telling him what I really wanted to do.

We ate in silence as we often did after a spat, and I shoved one or two fries into my mouth while discreetly scanning the water taxi dock area. It was hard to see from this distance, but I managed to make out that the taxi stands were buzzing with activity.

"Hon, if you don't mind, I'd like to take a walk by myself along the beach after lunch. Are you okay with that?"

"Don't you want company?"

"No, I'm fine. I just want to check out the beach shops." Peter hated souvenir shopping, and I knew that would deter him.

"Okay, but be careful. Don't wander too far past the resort grounds."

We finished our meals and the waitress asked if we wanted coffee.

"Black coffee for me," said Peter.

"None for me, thanks."

Again, Peter looked at me in surprise. "What? No coffee? You always have coffee after lunch."

"Hey, if you don't mind, I just really want to check out the souvenir shops now."

"Oh, I get it, you have shopping on your mind. Go ahead. I'm going to stay here and catch up with the news. Don't be long. You'll find me here when you come back."

I started for the shops but kept walking along the shoreline where the water taxis were moored. As I approached the docks, I spotted The Love Boat Captain alone on his boat. He was shirtless and was wearing mirrored aviator sunglasses. He looked like a young stud on the prowl.

"Excuse me," I said, calling for his attention.

He looked up immediately and removed his sunglasses in a slow, deliberate motion. Something I'm sure he had practiced many times before in front of a mirror.

"Welcome aboard, my lovely lady! Where can I take you today? Little French Key? Fantasy Island? *My* place? Anywhere you fancy, my beautiful."

"Sorry I'm not going anywhere today. I just want to ask you a question if you don't mind."

I stepped onboard and unlocked my phone to show him a picture of Julia, which I had pulled from the Roatan police website.

"Do you recognize her?"

He immediately perked up. He examined the photograph carefully and seemed to take an inordinate amount of time to respond even though I could see that he had immediately recognized Julia.

"Yes, I've seen her around. Why do you ask?"

"She's my friend and I can't get a hold of her. I really need to speak to her. Did you see her hanging around by any chance?"

I felt someone approaching me from behind. I looked to the side and saw in the corner of my eye The Love Boat Captain acknowledging his coworker with a nod. It was the elderly water taxi driver that I had spoken to earlier.

"Is everything alright?" the old man asked, trying to quickly ascertain what was going on.

I showed him the picture of Julia. "Have you seen my friend?"

"Yes, I believe I saw her earlier today," the old man said.

I could feel my heart beating hard. *My God, let this be true.*

"In fact, I saw her earlier this morning. She didn't want a ride. She walked to the edge of the dock and just stood there for a long time staring at the ocean. She was alone and seemed preoccupied. Anyway, she left a couple of hours ago heading for the resort."

For a moment I thought he was talking about Julia. Then I realized it was probably Cheryl he had seen on the docks. It all made sense to me now. I thanked the old man and turned my attention back to The Love Boat Captain.

"What about you? You said you've seen her around. When was that?"

"I just started my shift. I didn't see her today."

"Did you see her yesterday?"

"No, maybe the day before. I think during the night of my last shift."

"Did you talk to her?"

"Not much, she wasn't very chatty."

"Did you offer her a ride?"

"Yes, I gave her a ride. Why so many questions?"

I ignored his question and continued with my line of inquiry, "Where did you take her?"

He hesitated and looked at the old man as if to seek his approval. The old man nodded.

"Little French Key," he finally replied while putting his sunglasses back on.

"When you took her to Little French Key, was she alone?"

"Yes."

"What time was that?"

"Oh, it was late, we left the docks here well past eleven p.m."

I stared hard at him while absorbing and sorting out in my mind what I'd just learned. He did not seem comfortable. In fact, he looked somewhat nervous to me. He exchanged a couple of furtive looks with the old man, who had been watching us closely. Then he picked up his shirt, indicating that he had enough.

"Please believe me, miss, I know it was late for a woman to be alone in Little French Key, but she assured me she was meeting a friend. Now I've got work to do. Customers are waiting."

The old man, who had been witnessing the whole exchange quietly, glared at me and said, "Look lady, I told you I saw her today. Why are you asking where she was a few nights ago?"

"Because I don't think the woman you saw today was my friend. It was probably her twin sister. My friend is still missing."

What I said had a definite impact on them. They kept quiet for a moment, shaking their heads, staring at each other, and looking around for an excuse to walk away. It was obvious to me they had a hard time making up their minds about how to respond. And I was not about to help them. I thought it best to tell them as little as possible in order to find out if they were telling me the truth. Because if they were not hiding something, they were sure acting guilty.

Ultimately, it was the old man who felt compelled to say something. "I'm sorry about your friend, miss."

"Well, that's good, but it's not enough." Turning my attention to the so-called Love Boat Captain, I pointed my finger at him and said, "I think the police need to know that my friend Julia took a ride with you on your water taxi the night she was last seen."

The young water taxi driver was clearly shaken. "I'm sorry I gave a ride to your friend so late at night. It was against my better judgement. You have to believe me." He looked up at the old man, who was glaring at him. "But she begged me to take her. I warned her she shouldn't go alone. But she assured me her friend would be there to meet her. I'm so sorry. I hope nothing bad happened to her."

"I hope so, too, for your own sake. I think you should tell the police everything you know. And if I were you, I'd do it as soon as possible, Love Boat Captain, or whatever your real name is. The police will find out sooner or later. If you don't tell them yourself, you'll be in trouble."

I let my warning sink in while closely observing his reaction. He glanced at the old man seeking support. But the old man would have none of it. I let a minute or two pass and finally posed my most obvious question.

"When you dropped her off at Little French Key that night, did you see the friend she was meeting?"

"There were a few people at Little French Key that night...a couple of young kids fooling around. I asked her if her friend was there. She said yes. Then she paid me and left before I could say anything else."

"So you didn't see her friend. But did you at least watch where she went after she left your taxi?"

"No, because a young couple was already waiting on the dock and asked me for a ride. I left Little French Key right away with them onboard. They were my last customers that night.

I dropped them back at this dock and then went home for the night. That's all I know, I swear."

"Go tell the police what you just told me. They need to know what happened as soon as possible." My tone was firm and left no doubt about my meaning.

I left the two men thinking that I might have learned something important. Amongst all the facts I had uncovered, one issue in particular stood out in my mind. Were the water taxi drivers telling me the whole truth?

I had my suspicions. I pondered whether to trust the young driver with the information or go to the police myself. And of course, I had to do something about Peter, who was waiting for me at the beach bar restaurant. He would have many questions for me, but I was not in the mood to deal with him now. Deep in thought, I passed by our room and kept on walking until I reached Julia's room further down the hallway. It still had the police tape attached to the door. But for some reason the door was slightly ajar. I took a peek inside to see if someone was there. "Hello?" I called out cautiously.

"Hello, miss." I heard a deep voice behind me. It startled me, and I turned around. It was Officer Juan.

"You shouldn't be here, miss. This room is off-limits."

"Oh, sorry, the door was open and..." Feeling flustered, I stuttered, "Julia is my friend, and I was wondering if she was back in her room."

The police officer shook his head. "No, sorry. We still don't know where she is."

"Look, officer, I was just talking to one of the water taxi drivers. I showed him a picture of Julia, and he recognized her immediately. He said he gave Julia a ride in his taxi a couple of nights ago. He told me that he took her to Little French Key near the end of his night shift to meet a friend."

"Really? What's the name of the water taxi driver?" Officer Juan asked.

"I don't know his real name. He's the young one. He calls himself The Love Boat Captain."

"I know who you mean. His name is Miguel. I'll speak to him. Thank you, Misty."

Officer Juan walked away after locking the door behind him. I was surprised that he had made no mention of our earlier conversation in his office. At the time, he seemed very curious to know more about Peter's whereabouts the night Julia's was last seen. Yet, he did not broach the subject again. It was somewhat reassuring, as perhaps he did not think it was worth pursuing. But something in the back of my head was still nagging me. I was not entirely satisfied with how the search for Julia was proceeding.

Miguel seemed friendly enough, but he gave me the impression that he was holding something back from me. What exactly, I could not tell. It was just a feeling. Was he afraid of something or someone? Here again I was speculating.

Officer Juan was another matter altogether. I did not think that he was taking the disappearance of Julia seriously. He seemed to just be going through the motions. I wondered if the Caribbean *laissez-faire* attitude prevalent in the other islands had taken hold of Roatan as well. I could not comprehend, for instance, why he had not already interviewed Miguel. *Should he not have questioned all the taxi drivers on the island in the first place? Shouldn't that be part of a standard investigation? What was he really doing to find Julia?* I was glad that I got involved. But it bothered me to no end that I really didn't know what else to do. I felt so powerless and had no help.

Peter was not supportive, even forceful, deterring me from any involvement. Scott, on the other hand, was an enigma. His behavior was odd. He was snooty and self-centered most of the time. But in moments of crisis, he gave the appearance of care and genuine concern.

Our room was just a few doors away. I stepped in to sort out my thoughts. The room was tidy and the bed made, a huge contrast with what was going on in my world. I sat on the edge of the bed, thinking about all the things that had happened during our stay in Roatan. But above all, I felt guilty that I'd kept so many secrets from Peter. But the truth would have caused another argument. And I hated quarrels, especially with a loved one. Avoidance was not a solution either. The right thing to do was to talk to Peter. *Honesty is always best.*

The maid had left the window of our room slightly ajar. From the bed where I was resting, I could hear Peter's voice outside on the terrace. He must have returned to the room while I was on the docks enquiring about Julia. He was chatting with someone, but only his voice carried inside the room.

"I don't know what to think anymore."

He spoke in a barely audible voice, but the tone carried an undeniable strain.

"It'd be fine if only she would listen to me."

My curiosity got the better of me, I had to know who he was talking to. I jumped out of bed and tiptoed to the window. I saw Peter in the far end corner of the terrace. He was alone and seemed intense, pacing back and forth, the phone glued to his ear, to notice my presence.

"I know it should pass. But this time it seems different. The girl is gone, and Scott is the last one to have spent time with her."

Peter suddenly stopped pacing and turned facing me. I retreated immediately from the window and hid behind the curtains. I waited holding onto my breath as long as I could, praying that Peter had not seen me. I was rewarded by a long silence. After what seemed like an eternity, I dared another peek outside, careful not to be seen. Peter was listening intently to the person on the phone with him. He made a face at something that was said. The whole situation seemed surreal.

"I hope nothing serious happened to her. She should not have left the resort alone at night. I told her to be careful."

The person at the other end of the line said something that perturbed Peter even more. He clinched his teeth and rubbed his face. "No, I didn't tell the police that I spoke to her. And no, I didn't follow her. Who do you think I'm?" he shouted.

After a few more words, Peter cut the conversation short and headed for the door that gave access to the room. In one swift motion, I jumped back on the bed, hid my head under the blanket and feigned being asleep. What I just heard made me shiver.

I had no idea what to make of it.

CHAPTER 12

*Negativity serves no one. It only limits your
potential for happiness.*

ater that day, Peter was sitting alone
where I'd left him. He was busy scroll-
ing the screen of his phone with his index finger. I stood in front of him waiting for him to
take notice of me. It was time to speak the truth,
accept the consequences, and be satisfied with
my decision. I was ready to unburden myself no
matter what. The phone call that I overheard
was at the forefront of my mind, and needed to
be clarified. I was still waiting for Peter to pay
attention to me when I heard someone calling

my name. I turned around and saw Jen waving at me. She was heading in my direction, holding onto her floppy hat. I met her halfway, leaving Peter behind engrossed with his phone.

"Hi, Misty!" Jen greeted me with a smile.

I almost laughed in relief, welcoming the distraction. "Hi, Jen, how are you?"

"Just fabulous, thanks. Ben and I had lunch at one of the small restaurants at the far end of the beach. We had fresh seafood and great wine. It was absolutely delicious. You and Peter should try it sometime. I highly recommend it. Anyway, how are you?" She reached out for my hand and held it for a moment. It was a warm and comforting gesture, so innocent, yet so genuine. She emanated so much positive energy that it made it easy to talk to her.

"I'm okay. But...I just found out something very troubling about Julia. I was just about to tell Peter but, to tell you the truth, I'm glad you came over."

"Why is that?"

"Well as you know, it's just that Peter wants to stay clear of the search for Julia, and I'm sure he'll be angry if I tell him what I did."

Jen looked steadily at me. "So, what did you do? What did you find out?"

"I went over to the docks and spoke with a couple of water taxi drivers. I found out one of them had given a ride to Julia on his boat. He told me that he had taken her to Little French Key very late on the night that she was last seen."

"Oh, God bless her! Why would a woman venture alone over there late at night? I pray that no harm came to her. I've been thinking a lot about her since you told me she was missing. I was told that the island was safe, but I guess we never know. In any event, if you think it will start a fight with Peter, then you don't really need to tell him now, do you? Just tell the police and let them sort everything out."

"It's just that I don't think it's right to just ignore the fact that we don't know where she is, or if anything has happened to her. It worries me to death. I'm so grateful that I'm able to talk to you about it. I'm afraid that I'll lose my mind if I just keep burying the whole thing. Too many subjects are off-limits as far as Peter is concerned. He just wants me to avoid anything that could give me any stress. He thinks that it's his responsibility to protect me from having an anxiety attack. It's so frustrating that I can't mention anything to him about Julia. I find myself having to keep secrets from him. And..." I suddenly stopped speaking, no longer certain if I was telling Jen too much. *What would Peter say if he finds out?*

"And?" Jen asked.

"And...I don't know if I should tell you about my problems anymore. It's rather personal, and I don't want you to think badly of Peter and me."

"Misty, you are not the only one. Most couples struggle with a variety of issues over the course of their relationships. Ben and I..." She suddenly looked away and remained quiet for a few minutes. When she turned to face me, I saw her teary eyes staring at me. She wiped her face and in a soft broken voice, resumed what she wanted to tell me. "Not so long ago, Ben and I had some major disagreements. It got to a point that I almost left him. We've not resolved all of our issues yet, but we are both working at it. We came to Roatan in order to celebrate our renewed commitment to each other." She paused again, and this time, she smiled at me.

"I don't know what to say. I mean I'm sorry and happy for you at the same time."

"It's alright, Misty. Now let's talk about your issue. But it's all up to you. If you feel it would help, then maybe you should go ahead and tell me. You can trust me. After twenty-five years of marriage, believe me I've seen and heard it all. But if you're not comfortable telling me, it's fine with me too."

I observed Jen for a moment to consider what she had said. There was something about her that was so inviting. She seemed like a caring and honest person. It didn't take me long to make up my mind that I could trust her.

"Peter is going to wonder where I was this past hour. And if he finds out that I went over to talk to the water taxi drivers earlier today, he'll freak out. You see, he thought I went souvenir shopping. I can't keep lying to him, Jen."

"It's okay, Misty. Don't worry so much. You don't need to lie to him, but you don't need to tell him the whole truth either. He doesn't need to know all the details."

I knew that Jen was trying to be helpful, even though I didn't fully agree with her. You cannot build a healthy relationship based on half-truths or outright lies. That was what I strongly believed in. But I couldn't take it anymore—I had told Peter so many lies. Jen was right about one thing though, timing was everything. I'll tell Peter the whole truth at the right time. Just not now. First, the police needed more time to work on the information I'd given them. Something might come out of it, and then I'll talk to Peter. My mind was made up, and I thanked Jen.

Jen left to join her husband, and I walked back to see how Peter was doing. I found him still engrossed with his phone when I approached him.

"Hey, Peter," I said with a tap on his shoulder.

"Hi, sweetie." He looked up at me for a moment, smiled, and then looked down at his phone again and said, "How was your shopping?"

"It was alright, but I didn't find anything I liked."

Peter was not paying much attention to me and seemed more fascinated by what he was reading on his phone. I shook my head in tired amusement. "You know, Peter, I worked up quite a sweat, so I'm going to head back to our room and cool off for a while."

"Sounds good to me. I'll see you there later," he said, not bothering to look up at me. When he was focused on his phone like that, it was hard to get his full attention anyway. It worked to my benefit today. I honestly didn't know if I still had the will to tell him what I'd been doing while I was away.

I closed the door behind me and turned up the air conditioner. All the excitement of the day had taken its toll on my aching body. But my mind would not stop racing. Images of Little French Key kept flashing through my head. I could not explain it, and for some reason, I was not able to chase the images away. Frustrated, I grabbed my phone and did a Google search on the island news to see if anything relevant had been reported. That's when I noticed a text message I'd received from Nick at work: *Misty, check your email.*

I tapped open my email and there it was… NorthWealth was closing its doors. The news hit me hard. I knew the demise of NorthWealth was a matter of time. I just did not expect it so soon. I felt sick to my stomach. The email to the staff was written by our CEO, with regrets. *Regrets*…They needed staff to remain at work to wind down the business. They were offering retention bonuses. The closing date was set for the end of June. *What about severance?* There was no mention of it. Wow! This was big. I had been with the firm for ten years. I had been there when business was booming and growing. I had seen things turn for the worst so dramatically. It had been difficult, and so very stressful. Truth be told, I had really wanted to quit my job for quite some time. Peter and I had discussed it many times. I had been depressed about my job long before Peter and I had left for our trip. But I was not about to leave the firm without collecting my severance. The uncertainty of finding a new job was stressful enough.

I had mixed emotions about the whole thing. On one hand, I was glad a decision had finally been made. The uncertainty and speculation had been excruciating. There had been rumors that NorthWealth had interested buyers. Apparently, the firm had been very close to being sold more than a few times. But now it was bankrupt. *Will there be enough money left for severance? How will I be able to manage until I find a new job?* I knew that it wouldn't be easy in these uncertain economic conditions.

I had held onto that job because I could tell the end was near. I had banked on getting a large payout for my many years of service. But what if this was not to be? I lived alone and on a tight budget. I guess I could move in with Peter, but we hadn't had that talk yet. It was too soon in our relationship. And the way things were going between us lately, it gave me pause to reconsider. I needed to speak to Peter about it. He would have a plan and a solution. That was one of his best qualities. He could think clearly no matter how much pressure he was under. "The more pressure, the sharper I get," he often boasted to me.

The news about the demise of my company was deeply unsettling, particularly for what it meant to me and my colleagues. But I was convinced that it was not the end. New opportunities will present themselves eventually. I was sure of it. There was one thing I knew with greater certainty, life will go on for all of us. But what about Julia? Was she even alive?

My mind fell into a whirlwind of possibilities, consequences, expectations, and disappointments. One worry piling on top of another was simply too much for me to manage. I let out a few sobs and then a full-blown crisis hit me. I couldn't control my emotions as tears flowed freely down my cheeks. I covered my face with shaking hands and melted into deep loud sobs. My pulse kept racing, my chest tightened, and heart palpitations made my breathing difficult. I felt dizzy, and everything around me suddenly turned blurry. I felt the walls closing in on me. Panic was slowly setting in, and there was no one around to rescue me.

It took all the willpower I could muster for me not to fall into an uncontrollable anxiety attack. I let the time pass, focusing my mind on being present and taking deep breaths even if they were painful. I closed my eyes, not letting any negative thoughts enter my mind.

I did not know how long I had been in that state before I began to feel somewhat normal again. I had not felt so sick in months and swore to never, ever, neglect my meds again. I reached for a tissue but grabbed my phone instead. I remembered that I was about to do a Google search on Little French Key before the bad news about my company had hit me. There were tons of links. As I scrolled through them, one in particular caught my attention. It read: *"Woman Pulled from the Water at Little French Key...A woman was carried out of the water by a man earlier this week. The woman was without vital signs when paramedics administered first aid..."*

"Oh my God!" I gasped.

"Why is it so dark in here?"

Startled, I looked up and saw Peter standing over me. Sitting on the edge of the bed with phone in my hand and tears flowing down my cheeks, I didn't know what to say or where to begin, so I just blabbered, "I think Julia drowned!"

"What? Why would you think that?"

I handed Peter my phone and pointed my finger at the article. He must have read it at least twice, while I waited for him to speak. I could see his jaw clenched while he was reading the news clip. Something was wrong. This was not the reaction I was expecting.

He shook his head and stared steadily at me. "Misty, this article is from fifteen years ago! Why are you reading this?" I could hear the exasperation in his voice.

"What? Really? Let me see!" I grabbed the phone from his hands.

I swallowed hard. "Oh, my God you're right!"

"Misty, why are you still digging into something that does not concern you? I told you many times to leave this whole Julia thing alone."

"I'm sorry, Peter, but I can't stop worrying about her. I wanted to see if I could find any mention of her in the local news."

One look at Peter, and I knew this was going to turn into another fight. But as much as I hated arguing with him, I desperately wanted to tell him how I felt.

Peter took a couple of steps towards me and put his hands on my shoulders. He stared into my eyes. "Misty, you are obsessed with Julia. You have to let this go. There is nothing you can do that the police can't do better. I've told you that before. You're making yourself sick. I'm really concerned about what all this does to you."

With tears in my eyes I retreated, as usual. I told Peter he was right again. But I was not completely finished. From somewhere deep inside of me I managed to gather enough nerve to stammer, "Peter, there's more I need to tell you..."

He saw the anguish on my face, and he softened his tone when he spoke to me again. "What do you mean there's more? What else do you need to tell me?"

I did not answer right away. I needed time to think clearly. There was so much I'd kept hidden from him. I sat quietly, my arms crossed on my chest. Then I looked up at Peter. *Where to start?* Best to begin with the job news, I thought after a long internal struggle.

"Peter, I received an email from work. The office is closing."

"What?" Peter's eyes widened, and he seemed genuinely taken aback.

"It's okay, Peter... I mean, I will be okay." Peter didn't look convinced. He knew me too well.

"Peter, remember we talked about me leaving my job not so long ago. Remember what you told me then? It could be a new beginning, a fresh start, a clean break from all the tension, headaches, and stress this job has given me over all these years."

Peter nodded in agreement. "Yes, of course I remember. It's not the end of the world, you're right. With your skills, you'll find a better job in no time at all."

I took a deep breath. I could not believe that I was the one doing the reassuring after what had just happened. There was so much more I wanted to talk to him about. If only I could find the right time, the right way, to tell him the truth without causing another quarrel.

I swallowed hard, gathering the courage to spit it all out, but I was too overwhelmed by emotions. "My head is spinning Peter...I don't feel so good...Please give me a minute." I put my hand on my forehead, and Peter kneeled in front of me.

"It's okay, hon, take all the time you need. Everything is going to work out just fine. You'll see. You'll find a better job."

He sat down beside me at the edge of the bed and began to gently rub my back.

"Maybe you should take an extra dose of your medication. You are under extreme stress. It will make you feel better."

I began to cry, and in between sobs I managed to utter, "Peter, I forgot to bring my anti-anxiety medication with me on this trip."

Peter stopped rubbing my back. He clenched his fist and swallowed hard while staring up at the ceiling fan.

"Misty, how could you forget your medication?"

Tears that were welling up in my eyes began to trickle down my cheeks. I felt so helpless. I had delayed the inevitable for so long, and now that it was done, I was so ashamed. Peter was furious with me, and I could not blame him. I waited and waited for Peter to speak again. Not a word came out of his mouth. Instead, a deathly silence filled the room. No longer able to contain himself, Peter grabbed his key, headed for the door, and slammed it behind him.

I was feeling awful already...about losing my job, not having brought my meds with me, lying about it to Peter, and tormenting myself about the disappearance of Julia to top it all. And now I felt even worse that Peter was angry with me because I'd not been honest with him. I held my head in my hands and wept...and wept. Exhausted, I finally collapsed on the bed and cried myself to sleep.

I fell into a deep sleep and soon I began dreaming I was floating in the ocean on a raft. The motion of the waves was cradling me. It was strangely comforting, rocking back and forth as a warm breeze caressed my skin. I was feeling weak but somehow, I found the strength to sit up on the raft. I gazed out into the vast expanse of the ocean and felt my loneliness. Solitude was my only companion, and for a strange reason, it fulfilled my need at the time. There was a large land mass in the distance, but it was getting smaller and smaller before it eventually disappeared completely from the horizon.

I must have slept for a while, and when I finally woke up, the sun had penetrated the room. I felt rested and peaceful—a strange outcome in light of the recent events. I remained in bed for some time seeking warmth and comfort. After a while, feeling restless again, I reached for my phone. I had new messages. My heart fluttered. I'd received a long WhatsApp message from my sister. *God knows I love her, but I just can't deal with her now. She means well. But she will have a million questions and be quick to tell me what I should do.*

I typed a short and curt reply: *Let's chat when I get back.*

I refused to deal with any more bad news. I threw the phone on the bed and grabbed what I needed for the beach. I was about to rush out of the room but stopped myself at the last minute in front of the door. I couldn't resist giving another glance at my phone. The sight of it made me tense, but I grabbed it anyway, like a safety buoy.

I walked over to the pool area and found the only empty lounge chair. I threw my bag and towel on the chair and went straight for a swim. I got into a slow rhythm, feeling conscious of my movement in the water, taking time between each stroke. I could feel my arms push against the water's resistance, my feet kicking hard, and my breath slow and even. I swam at a steady pace and with purpose until I reached the far end of the infinity pool. I pulled myself up to the ledge facing the ocean. I took my time to enjoy the view and rested my eyes on the shimmering waves. A sea of sunbathers blanketed the beach, and the sun was beating hard on all the well-oiled bodies. One woman in particular running towards the water caught my attention. She was about to dive in the water. I watched her closely, the unmistakable sense that I had seen this woman somewhere before began to needle me.

I watched her swim against the current. One or two powerful strokes later she passed well beyond the halfway mark of the swimming area, which was cordoned by safety buoys. Curious, I pulled myself out of the pool, grabbed my towel, and headed for the sandy beach. At that point I heard the sharp whistle of the lifeguard and saw that the woman was swimming well past the lifebuoys. High waves were towering over her, but that did not seem to hinder her in the least. She just kept pace, cutting through the waves with no regard to how far she had gone. All along, the lifeguard was frantically waving for the woman to get back inside the safe area. At long last, she made a sharp turn and began to swim back towards the beach. A few more strokes, and she finally emerged from the water and started to walk back on the beach. I immediately recognized her. It was Cheryl. By the time I was able to reach her, she had already dried herself and was lying down on her towel.

Standing over her, I called out her name. "Hi, Cheryl. I was watching you swim from the pool. I didn't know that you were such a strong swimmer?"

Cheryl considered me for a moment. "I guess I'm not too bad. I've to thank my parents for that. They were awesome swimmers and made a point of teaching us how to swim at a very young age."

"It was a bit dangerous what you did. Don't you think so?"

"Oh, I was in no danger, believe me. I'm sorry if I gave a heart attack to the lifeguard."

"Poor fellow, I don't think he has recovered yet." We both laughed at our jokes.

"But seriously, Cheryl. How are you doing? Any news about your sister?"

Cheryl looked down and shook her head. Her features were troubled.

"I'm so sorry. Is there anything I can do to help?"

"No, but thank you for asking. I don't know what to do anymore. Wait and pray, I guess."

"It's not easy, I understand. You mustn't give up. She'll turn up safe and sound, I'm sure."

"Thank you so much, Misty. Your words of encouragement mean a lot to me."

I saw the tears starting to roll down on Cheryl's face, and I thought it was best to change subjects. "Can I ask you a question, Cheryl?"

"Sure. What is it?"

"Is this your first time in Roatan?"

"No, I've been in Roatan a couple of times when I was young. My parents were serious scuba divers, and this was their diving Mecca."

She smiled at the memory.

"I would watch them dive from the beach, but I was never allowed to go with them. I was too young, they told me, and so I would wait for hours for them to return. My father had an underwater camera and took breathtaking pictures of what he called the underworld. They loved to talk about their dives, and I always wished I was old enough to go with them."

Cheryl looked away, and I could see that she was fighting back tears. "My mother died when I was twelve," she suddenly let out in one breath.

"Oh, I'm so sorry. I didn't know. It must have been awful for you and your sister. You were so young."

"Yes. It was a difficult time for all of us. And my father...I'm sorry to say, was not always there to take care and console us. His way of dealing with his grief was to work all the time. My sister and I were left alone a lot. I wished that dad didn't have to work so hard so he could be home with us. Each time he left for work, we felt like we were being abandoned. It was like being an orphan."

Cheryl stopped speaking to wipe her eyes. I sensed she wanted to tell me more. I could relate to her need to talk to someone. So, I remained silent, giving her time to recover.

"Thank God for Julia," she said and began to cry again. "When my father went to work, she was always there for me. We kept each other company as we had no one else to turn to.

Sometimes my father would go away on business trips for days at a time. Julia would read me stories to help me fall asleep. She was always the strong one. She once told me that our father was acting that way because he didn't want to cry in front of us. *The death of our mother had broken something inside of him*, she said. So, he would hide behind his work and, when he could no longer cope with the pain, he would leave on those damn business trips. Our father never liked to show any emotion in front of us. He thought it was a sign of weakness, something to be ashamed of. All I have is Julia. I can't bear the thought of losing her!" Her voice was trembling, her body was shaking. She rested her head on my shoulder and kept sobbing.

I took her in my arms and hugged her tight for a long time, waiting for her sobs to subside.

Cheryl was so much like her sister. Her looks, her mannerisms, her voice, her hair, and the way she looked straight at you in the eyes were so much like Julia. There were nevertheless some very subtle differences between them.

I'd once read that even in the case of identical twins, they could have distinct temperaments. There was always a dominant sibling, and I'd no doubt that Julia was the one in this instance.

Cheryl's sudden appearance in Roatan showed that she obviously cared a lot about her sister. She was here to help find her, she had said. But she did not seem very engaged in the process, relying instead solely on the police. The effectiveness of the local police was a point of contention between Peter and me. The evidence, or more likely, the lack of evidence of progress so far in the search for Julia convinced me that more needed to be done.

"It's going to be alright, Cheryl. We're going to find Julia."

"God, I hope so," replied Cheryl meekly.

"In the meantime, keep your spirits up, and don't hesitate to let me know if there's anything I can do for you?"

"Talking helps."

"I wish I could find her for you."

Cheryl nodded and laid down beside me.

"Thanks, Misty." She reached for my hand and held it firmly. Her tight grip conveyed a need for comfort and support. Something that was sorely lacking in my life right now. I sat beside her until she became quiet and fell asleep.

CHAPTER 13

"There is a crack in everything, that's how light gets in."

—Leonard Cohen

I glanced at Cheryl sleeping beside me. She seemed at peace, but I knew better. Her life had been shattered by the tragic death of her mother. And now she was worried sick that she may have lost her sister too. As for me, I needed to sort out my issues with Peter. The spat we had earlier that morning was not entirely his fault. I shared a large part of the blame, and I did not fault him for being angry with me. I had to find a way to make things work better between us.

Otherwise, I had the feeling that our relationship could be irrevocably broken. *Life can be so complicated.*

I stood up, stretched my arms, and headed for the edge of the water. The tide was low, and I had to walk further than I intended. I wanted to dip my toes in the water to cool me down. The air was still, and as always, the sun was in full force. On my way down the beach, I saw Scott lying on the wet sand letting the waves roll over his body. I caught a glimpse of him staring at me, but he immediately looked away. *It was for the best after all*, I thought. All I wanted was for him to help me find Julia. But he had shut me down. His attitude hurt me and made me suspicious about his motivations.

I kept walking along the shoreline, soaking my feet and enjoying my freedom. It had been a while since I had seen Peter. I felt guilty having lied to him so many times. And I was even more distressed that I'd not yet found the courage to lay it all out once and for all. All of a sudden, Peter's voice pulled me out of my reflections.

"There you are!" Peter had a deep voice that carried far. He was walking fast in my direction. I stopped, assuming he was looking for me, only to realize that he was, in fact, making his way to speak to Scott.

I didn't think Peter noticed me observing him on the beach. Scott, who had been soaking in the sun, looked up when he heard Peter's voice. Peter knelt down beside Scott and spoke to him. They were very animated and looked like they were involved in an intense argument. I didn't want Peter to see me, so I retreated slowly away from the shoreline. I glanced back a few times, wishing I could hear what they were arguing about. Scott looked the more agitated of the two. He yelled something at Peter, but the roar of the waves made it impossible for me to hear what he'd said. Peter had his hands resting on his knees and just kept nodding his head in agreement. After a while Scott seemed to calm down. I knew then that Peter was doing his best to defuse the situation. Peter had a way of making you believe everything would be alright, if you just stop to think through the issues rationally, leaving all emotions on the side.

I kept watching them for a while. They were so engrossed in their conversation that they never noticed me observing them at a distance. Scott shook his head smiling, and I knew at that instant that Peter had won the argument. I continued walking along the beach with my flip-flops in my hands. It was a particularly hot day, and my feet throbbed sinking into the scorching sand. I moved deeper into the water, submerging my feet to ankle level. It was a mindless walk, and before long I found myself approaching the water taxi docks.

Miguel, The Love Boat Captain, was busy cleaning the inside of his little boat with a rag. I stopped for a moment, watching him get his boat ready for the next customer. Pleased with his work, he looked up, and we made eye contact. He waved at me to come aboard, and I got the feeling that something was afoot.

"Hi, miss. Did you find your friend?"

"No," I replied, clearly disappointed.

"I was hoping to speak to you, miss, but I didn't know how to find you."

"Why? Do you know something about my friend?"

"I just came back from Little French Key. While I was there, my buddy who works on the ferry told me about an incident that happened a couple of days ago. He said that a woman drowned in the rough waters. Apparently, she was swimming alone, late at night. A group of kids were partying there at the time, and one guy saw her go under. He rushed to her rescue and was able to pull her to the shore. They tried to revive her and called for help. She was unconscious the whole time. When the ambulance came, they took her to the local health centre."

"Oh my God! Could it be Julia?" My heart began to race, and I held onto the side of the boat to steady myself. "Did you tell Officer Juan?"

Miguel grunted loudly. "Not yet. I haven't had the chance, but I will soon."

"You should tell him what you know, right now. It could be very important. I have his number on my phone. Let's call him right away." I fumbled through my bag to find my phone. "Here's the number! Let me connect you to him and put you on speakerphone."

I tapped the contact call button on my phone, and after two rings, Officer Juan answered.

"Officer Juan here," he said in his usual no-nonsense tone.

"Officer Juan, this is Misty. I'm a guest at the Infinity Bay Resort. I spoke to you earlier today about Julia, the missing woman."

"Yes, Misty, I remember you. I'm sorry to tell you we have not found your friend yet."

"I'm with someone who may have some relevant information for you."

I held the phone closer to Miguel and invited him to speak.

"Hello officer, my name is Miguel."

"I know who you are, Miguel, the so-called Love Boat Captain. Don't waste my time and tell me what you know. Make it quick, I'm on my way out the door."

"Officer Juan, my friend who runs the ferry at Little French Key just told me that a woman drowned there a couple of nights ago. The woman was pulled from the water and was taken away by water ambulance. I just thought you might want to know in case you were not aware of this accident."

Officer Juan did not speak for a moment. Miguel raised his shoulders as he waited for a response. "Humm, no one told me that someone got into trouble in Little French Key. I'll look into it. Thank you, Miguel. Please hand the phone over to Misty."

Miguel gave me back my phone with a smirk on his face. *What an arrogant guy*, I thought as I grabbed my phone from his hands and took it off speakerphone.

"Thank you, Misty, for bringing this matter to my attention. It could be very helpful. I'll contact the health center immediately. I don't know why they didn't inform the police, but I'll find out what's going on and let you know."

"Thank you, officer. I'd really appreciate that. Glad to be of some help."

I have to talk to Cheryl... We may have found Julia.

"Miss, are you okay?" Miguel was staring at me. He had a concerned look on his face.

I shrugged. "I'm just thinking. I don't know what to make of all of this?"

"Don't worry so much, miss. The police will let us know soon enough."

"Yes...I suppose you're right. I have to go now Miguel. Thank you for telling me about this accident at Little French Key."

Please God, let Julia be alive.

I met Julia for the first time a few days ago. It was a brief encounter. A few words here and there, a matter of knowing where we were from, how long we will be staying in Roatan, and whether this was her first visit to the island. Nothing particularly meaningful, the sort of things strangers on vacation talk about. Yet ever since her sudden disappearance, I could not stop thinking about her.

Why was that?

I told myself that it was because I cared a lot about other people and worried when I thought something might happen to them. That was true most of the time. But with Julia something else was at play. I've often been puzzled as to why communication came so easily with certain people and not others? Why did we feel at ease right away with some people we hardly knew a moment earlier? Why a meeting of the mind, a complicity, could be established with no apparent effort with a total stranger. I have often struggled with these questions, and my inability to find adequate answers have always baffled me. But there was one thing I was absolutely certain of. I needed to find Julia in order to seal and build on the connection we had formed during our first encounter. In Julia, I saw a kindred spirit calling for my help.

I climbed out of the water taxi, leaving Miguel behind to tend to his business. My emotions were raw. I walked to the end of the dock and glanced in the direction of the resort at the far end of the beach. I needed more time to absorb the news and proceeded instead to walk the opposite way. The noon sun was sweltering, and before long, my entire body was covered in sweat, and I started to feel dizzy. I tried to reorient myself, searching for a spot in the shade, when luckily, a few steps away, I found the restaurant where Peter had taken me for my birthday.

I stepped inside where it was cool and comfortable. A young woman suddenly appeared. from the back of the kitchen

"Sorry, we're closed for lunch today and don't open until six for dinner."

"That's okay. Can I trouble you for a bottle of water? I'm not feeling well."

"Sure, honey, I'll be right back."

I felt lightheaded. The table where Peter and I ate dinner on my birthday was a few steps in front of me. I started walking, but before I could reach the chair my eyes went blurry and then my legs gave way.

"Miss, miss!" I heard a woman's voice. I managed to lift my head, the whole room was spinning, and my mind was in a total haze.

"Are you okay, miss?" the young lady asked again.

"Yes, I think so. What happened? I remember walking from the docks to this place, and I don't know what happened after that. I guess I must have passed out. What's wrong with me?"

"You fainted, miss. You're probably very dehydrated. You have to be careful with the sun in Roatan. This is the tropics, and the sun is not forgiving. Please have some water and drink it slowly. It will make you feel better."

I was thankful for the water and drank a few sips from the bottle she had given me. My mind was still foggy. The water seemed to help, but I felt tired and needed to rest some more. I drank more water, and after a while, feeling somewhat better, I tried getting up. but my legs felt weak and unsteady.

"Easy there, miss. Please take your time. You've not fully recovered yet."

"I'm fine now. Really. Sorry to trouble you."

"Oh, don't worry about it, honey. It's not the first time a tourist has passed out on this island," she said while holding onto my arm, making sure I was steady on my feet. Finally reassured about my condition, she asked me if I was from Canada.

"Yes, how did you know?"

"We get a lot of Canadian tourists," she said smiling.

I was beginning to feel much better and remembered that this was the second time I'd passed out in Roatan. *I have to learn to respect the Caribbean sun.*

"Look, I think I've taken enough of your time. Thank you so much for your help." I fumbled in my purse searching for some change to give her.

"Don't worry about it. Take your time and stay as long as you'd like. Don't mind me if I get back to the kitchen. Just shout if you need anything."

I touched my forehead to see if I had a fever. It felt fine, but my head kept pounding, and I knew that I needed more time to rest. My first thought was to call Officer Juan, as soon as I felt better. But I rejected the idea right away. He had promised to call me back as soon as he had some news. *God, I hope Julia is safe.*

Then I thought about Peter. I couldn't help myself from wondering what his conversation with Scott was all about. It had to be important, judging by Scott's spirited reaction. It also did not take me long to reject the idea of calling him. I was in no condition to have another squabble with him.

I took a few tentative steps, and while feeling slightly unsteady, I managed to walk back to the resort. Along the way I saw Roatan under a different light. This little island was so beautiful but looked and felt different somehow from when we first arrived. I realized that it was a place where people lived, not just a paradise for vacationers. It moved to its own beat while letting tourists borrow its natural charm and pristine beauty for the briefest of times. In some way, Roatan had kept a secret hidden from us. Under its idyllic beauty, a troubled past had been buried. As a colony, life could not have been easy for the original inhabitants of the island, kept under constant close watch by foreign occupiers. But somehow, the locals had managed to keep the faith over the years, in the hope that better times were to come. Indeed, life in Roatan had meaning. Perhaps I was too busy with all my worries that seemed to follow me everywhere to fully appreciate its significance. The young lady at the restaurant did not hesitate to help a total stranger. *I must remember to keep the faith.*

I passed by a young mother playing with her child in the sand. Another boy was building a sandcastle nearby. Couples were strolling along the beach. A frisbee fell on someone's head, and everyone laughed. The beach was full of happy people. I was flying back home in a couple of days and wondered if I could ever find the time to make up for what I'd been missing. As I was getting closer to the resort, I started looking for Cheryl, but she was no longer where I'd left her. Peter and Scott were still chatting away in the same spot where I'd seen them earlier in the day. I walked past them, just far enough away so they wouldn't notice me. I was still not ready to talk to them.

At the beach bar, guests were happily drinking, taking an early lead on happy hour. I continued walking along the pool area, hiding behind my sunglasses, wanting to be just an observer for now. Seeing what could have been.

I remembered the time we spent at Little French Key. It was a beautiful day, indeed. There we met Ben and Jen, a nice, friendly couple, on a vacation gifted to them by their son, Eddy. They had faced adversity of their own with a son who grew up with MS. And yet they seemed so well adjusted to their misfortune. A mindset that has not yet been fully embraced by Peter.

I've often wondered how perfect strangers could one day cross your path, and leave you with an indelible insight into your life. Divine interference, fate, or simply coincidence, all possibilities to which I've never been able to find a satisfactory answer. The message was clear though. If I could not be cured of my predicament, Peter better start being more accepting and stop trying to constantly shelter me.

I felt tears of sadness envelop me. *Oh no, here I go again.*

I needed to hide somewhere where no one could see me like this. I finally reached the guests' rooms, which were lined up in a straight row along a long corridor. It felt like the refuge I was looking for. Cool, quiet, and orderly, the long corridor helped me calm down. I stopped in front of Julia's room. I noticed that her window's curtains were slightly open. I made sure that no one was around and peered through the little opening. The room was plunged in semidarkness, but I was able to distinguish a few items inside amongst the shadows. The bed was made, and from the little I was able to see, the room seemed tidy. An open suitcase was on the floor against the wall with clothes folded neatly inside. There was a chair next to the suitcase with a soiled towel hanging on the armrest. This picture seemed odd to me. What was a soiled towel doing there if no one is using the room?

"Good day, ma'am!" A cheerful voice from behind startled me. I turned around to find a maid in her resort uniform and holding a small stack of towels.

"Oh, hello," I said, doing my best to sound natural.

"Can I help you, ma'am?"

"Oh no, thank you. I was trying to get some shade, it's so hot today," I said, hiding behind my best innocent smile.

The maid seemed satisfied with my explanation and continued on her way. I took a deep breath of relief after she left and proceeded immediately down the long corridor heading for our room. In front of the door, I searched for the keys inside my large beach bag. I had trouble finding them among the large amount of junk I always carried in the bag. Out of frustration I looked down the hallway hoping to find the maid, and that's when I saw a woman standing in front of Julia's room. From where I was standing, I couldn't exactly make out who the woman was, although there was something awfully familiar about her. I was about to walk over to her when the woman opened the door and quickly stepped into the room.

I was left alone in front of my room without my keys. *What to do?*

"Misty!" I turned around, and there was Peter walking towards me. "Hey, where have you been?"

I spoke hurriedly. "I went for a long walk."

"I was worried about you! You were gone a long time! Where did you go?"

Peter stared me down. "I just walked along the beach and stopped at Vintage Pearl, but the restaurant is not open during the day. So I came back."

"Why didn't you text me?"

"Sorry, I guess I lost track of time."

"Misty, do me a favor, next time you decide to disappear for several hours, tell me where you're going and text me if you're running late, okay?"

"Okay, Peter. I got it, sorry. What's the big deal, anyway?"

"Do I need to remind you that a woman from our resort is missing!"

I did not answer right away. I had no strength to argue, so I pretended to search in my bag.

"Misty, why are you just standing here, outside our room?"

"Because I can't find my key! Can you please open the door for me?" My tone was clear enough. I wanted to end this discussion.

Peter grinned, then pulled the room key from his back pocket. I rushed inside and headed straight for the washroom, slamming the door behind me. I ran the tap water and held onto the sink with shaking hands. I splashed cold water on my face and once I felt more composed, I opened the washroom door expecting to see Peter, but he was no longer in the room.

I poured myself a glass of water and drank it slowly. The emotional highs and lows of the day had taken their toll, and I had no energy left in my body. I laid down on my side of the bed, positioned my pillow comfortably under my head and immediately drifted into a deep sleep.

I dreamt about Julia and Cheryl. We were all together on a small boat, the size of a water taxi. We were having fun, chatting and enjoying the ride. The two sisters started singing "*Row, row, row your boat,*" and we all burst out laughing. Meanwhile, our little boat was drifting away and before we could do anything about it, we found ourselves lost in the middle of the ocean. All of a sudden, a huge wave hit our boat, lifting it high into the air, and almost flipping it over. The impact was so forceful that both sisters fell into the water. I managed somehow to hold onto the boat. Julia and Cheryl were both struggling in the water to stay afloat. I reacted quickly, I had to save them. I jumped in the water, and both sisters grabbed onto me at once. We were all about to drown, and I had to make a quick decision. I had enough strength to save only one sister. I woke up suddenly in sweats screaming. The dream felt so real and vivid.

Why can't my mind take a break? I just want peace in my life.

I could hear the muttered sound of Peter's voice. I reached for him in the bed, but he wasn't there. The room was dark except for a crack of light shining through the curtains. I got up from the bed and took a peek outside through the gap in the curtains. Peter was sitting outside on the small terrace in front of our room, chatting with Scott. There were a few empty cans of beer on the small side table. They were both laughing and seemed to be enjoying themselves. I reached for my phone to see if Officer Juan had left me any messages. There were none. I wanted to call him but chose instead to text him for fear that Peter would hear me. I composed a simple message:

Officer Juan, it's Misty. Do you have any news? Is it Julia who nearly drowned at Little French Key the other night? Is she safe? I pressed send and waited anxiously for the response.

A few minutes passed. Then my phone lit up with a message from Officer Juan.

Misty, a woman was indeed taken to the local health centre a couple of nights ago. She pulled through, and she is okay. They wanted to keep her for observation as she was a bit confused. But she discharged herself the next day. She told the nurse she wanted to go back to her resort, and then fly home in a couple of days. She said her name was Rose but wouldn't tell where she was staying.

I read the message over several times. I was so relieved to hear that the woman was safe. But the message said that the woman's name was Rose and made no mention of Julia. *What does it mean?* I quickly texted Officer Juan another message.

Thank you for the update, Officer Juan. I am so relieved to hear the woman is fine and safe. What about Julia?

I waited a very long time for a reply but none came. I lay down in bed, holding onto my phone, hopelessly waiting for a response. I put the ringer on vibrate and looked at the time. The night had settled in. I was quite exhausted and began to doze off once again.

Be patient.

CHAPTER 14

A white cotton dress for the soul.

I woke up this morning, feeling strange. Nothing weird or far out, just a strong impulse for something different. I was in the mood for a little adventure. Something out of the ordinary. Something that did not involve Peter, Scott, Cheryl, or Julia for that matter. I was not being irrational. I only wished that all my worries would go away, if I distanced myself from them all.

I took my time getting dressed that morning, looking at the very back of the closet for something to wear that I had yet worn on this trip. That was a start. Now I needed to think of something to do all by myself. The resort offered yoga lessons by the pool. There was also a bike tour around the island. I chose a self-guided walking tour in town. I grabbed my bag and left a note for Peter to let him know what I was doing. I told him to have fun, and not to worry about me.

The concierge recognized me right away and called a taxi for me. He asked if Peter would be joining me. I thought the question was odd. What was he implying? Like a perfect gentleman though, he opened the door of the cab for me and waved at me as we were driving away.

The taxi dropped me off in the middle of the shopping district in the center of town. I paid the driver, who inquired when he should come back to take me back to the resort. I told him I did not have a clue, so he gave me his business card.

"Just call me when you're ready, ma'am," he said in broken English as he drove away.

Now what? I was in town all by myself, and I had no idea where to go or what to do. A fellow on a motorcycle stopped dangerously close to me to ask me if I wanted a ride and have some fun. I could not believe my ears. Everyone seemed so forward with me because I was a woman walking alone. Not that I minded the attention, but I came to town for a break, not for another set of headaches.

The center of town possessed all the charm and attractions that would appeal to tourists from the great north. Little cafés with welcoming verandas shielded from the sun by large brightly colored parasols, gift shops everywhere offering a full gamut of knickknacks, and a constant humming of Latin music in the background.

It was a pleasant change from the sanitized amenities of the resort. I immediately liked what I saw. And I did not feel guilty that I was enjoying it all by myself. I started to roam around the area and decided to check out the first store that displayed clothing hooked on hangers on the wall on either side of the door. I took a quick peek inside. The little store was packed from floor to ceiling with all sorts of goods: hats, purses, beach towels with full-length-sized prints of muscular men and half naked women, sandals, and beautiful cotton dresses. A good-looking young man got up as soon as he saw me peeking inside. He stared at me with alluring dark brown eyes and invited me to come in.

"Come in. Please come in, miss. Take your time to look inside. We've lots of beautiful merchandise for you, beautiful lady," he said with a broad grin.

His smile was infectious, and I could detect that he was checking me out with his eyes roaming all over my body. He was bold about it. I was flattered, I could not deny it. He saw me hesitating, and he right away pulled a white cotton dress from a rack beside him.

"This dress was made for you. Why don't you try it on, miss?"

He was right. The dress was exquisite, especially designed to flatter the body of any woman in all the right places. Not necessarily something I would wear back home but definitely a dress meant for a happy time on a sunny vacation.

"Try it on, miss," he said while inviting me to come to the back of the store, where a cubicle hidden by a black curtain served as the change room. I hesitated for a moment. He kept staring at me with his big brown eyes, and I finally gave in. *The dress is simply too beautiful*, I told myself. I grabbed the dress and headed straight to the back of the store. The change room was not bigger than the tiniest of closets, and the curtain provided just enough privacy to cover an average person above waist level. I'd removed my blouse when suddenly I saw the face of the young man peeping inside, out of a corner of the curtain.

"How does the dress fit, miss? Do you need any help?"

I was shocked, frightened, and excited all at the same time. He saw me watching him. He did not move and kept staring at me. I do not know how long I stayed half crouched, holding on dearly to my top over my breast, when I finally managed to find my voice and screamed, "Get out. Go away."

He tossed me a broad grin and muttered something in Spanish under his breath. The only words I could make out were *"bella" and "preciosa."*

I immediately slipped on my top and without a word I sprinted out of the store as fast as I could. Once in the open air, I took a deep breath and walked away. I wandered around the area for a long time. Nothing seemed to hold my interest any more. I kept walking aimlessly and somehow, I ended up where I started from—the infamous store. The young man was standing on the sidewalk in front of his shop. He smiled when he saw me, proud of himself like he had been expecting me. He followed me inside and stood close behind me. I could feel his breath on my neck, which gave me shivers. I managed to mumble "I'd like to get the dress."

"Would you like to try it on first this time?"

I glanced at the change room at the very back of the store.

"No, thank you," I said with as much authority in my voice I could muster. It was a spontaneous, out of character decision to buy a dress without trying it on first. So be it, I had to have it.

"I'll take the dress."

He tossed me another smile in response. He was toying with me.

"Please come back again. We've got lots of pretty blouses and dresses." He put the white cotton dress in a bag and handed it over to me with a smug look.

That was the extent of my newfound freedom for a day. When I returned to the resort, Peter was waiting for me in the lobby.

"How was your day, sweetheart?" He asked.

"Pleasant and uneventful," I said.

Another secret.

CHAPTER 15

"Nothing diminishes anxiety faster than action."

—Walter Anderson

I must have slept soundly that night. When I woke up, Peter was lying beside me. I didn't even remember him coming to bed. I reached for my phone to see the time. It was six o'clock, at least thirty minutes before the sound of the alarm. My little escapade yesterday had been refreshing, even if the upshots did not last long. The white cotton dress was a success. Peter absolutely loved it on me. I did not tell him the details of my encounter with the shopkeeper, as I did not see the point of that. I was hoping there would be a text reply from Officer Juan, but there wasn't. I was restless and decided to get up and shower before Peter woke up. I let the water run all over my body, keeping my eyes closed in the hope it would clear my mind and relax me. But I was still apprehensive about hearing from Officer Juan, and I worried about how my morning conversation with Peter would go. I decided to greet him with a smile no matter what. *Better start the day on a positive note.* And of course, I wouldn't dare mention anything about Julia and definitely not a word about the drowning incident at Little French Key.

I was very careful not to make any noise when I opened the washroom door. Peter was asleep, and I was not sure what to do. If I left the room without waking him up, he would accuse me of disappearing again. I wrestled with the idea for a moment and finally made up my mind. *So be it.* I gathered the courage to leave the room as quietly as possible. I tiptoed across the room to the door, slowly turned the knob, but to my dismay the door was stuck. I pulled it as hard as I could, and it finally gave way, but unfortunately, not without making a loud squeaky noise.

"Hey! You're up already? Where are you going?"

"Oh, you startled me! I thought you were asleep!"

"Not anymore! Are you about to abandon me again?" Peter said with a wide grin.

"Look, honey, I just need some air. I was just going to sit outside on the terrace of the resort for a bit."

"Okay, enjoy!" Peter turned his back to me and pulled the covers over him.

I was pleasantly surprised by the way he had reacted. He did not seem to mind that I was about to sneak out on him. I studied Peter carefully, feeling somewhat guilty. I was not the easiest person to be with. That was not something I consciously chose to be. I had my moments like everyone. But my bad feelings seemed to linger longer. Peter had a right to expect more out of me. He was not the cause of my recurring angst. His intentions were good for the most part, even if his methods left a lot to be desired.

I reminded myself that guilt was only an emotion, just like joy and affection. It was a matter of choosing well between which emotions to hold on to, and which bad feelings to let go. *If only it were that easy.* I knew that my sense of guilt was the byproduct of my troubled mind. And that was what I needed to resolve first. I gave Peter a bright smile, even though he could not see me under the blanket and shut the door behind me.

Morning was my favorite part of the day. Early risers like me were rewarded with the majestic beauty of the resort without the noise and constant buzz of activity around the pool area. The morning was also my best time to do some serious thinking.

A blast of hot air hit me hard as soon as I stepped outside. *Thank God for the ocean breeze,* I smiled at the thought. It made the scorching morning sun just bearable. But then it did not take me long to feel lightheaded again. This time

I knew it was neither the heat nor dehydration that caused me to feel that way. It was anxiety. I knew that something was not working between Peter and me. At times, it felt like I was walking on eggshells. Something had to be done about it soon. And the sooner, the better.

I looked around, taking stock of my surroundings. I could hear the ocean calling me. I was tempted to run to the beach, dive into the water, and let the waves carry me afar. But then I may be accused of disappearing again. *Am I being ridiculous?* It was a self-created quandary, which had happened to me often on this trip.

Julia's room was not far from where I was standing. I wondered if the room was occupied by someone else. Perhaps Cheryl had moved into her sister's room. It was too tantalizing, I had to find out.

I walked over to Julia's room and tried to peek inside through the window. I had no luck this time. Someone had pulled the curtains tightly closed. I knew I was being nosy, and I walked away still feeling restless. I picked up my phone to see if there were any messages from Officer Juan. Still nothing.

The more I thought about it, the more I was convinced that the woman who had almost drowned at Little French Key had to have been Julia. Who else could it be? She was there that night.

I was halfway down the hallway when I heard a noise behind me. Someone was standing in the doorway in front of Julia's room. I stared at the shadow trying to make out who it could be. The woman turned to face me. Our eyes locked for an instant. But my eyes were not yet accustomed to the darkness in the hallway. I could only make out the silhouette of a tall woman. The woman pushed her long dark hair away from her face. I gasped with my mouth wide open and stammered her name.

"Julia! Is that you?"

She smiled shyly. "Yes. Hello, Misty."

"I am so relieved to see you. Are you okay? Where have you been? We were all so worried about you?" I had a million questions, and I just kept on talking and probing relentlessly for more answers.

"Slow down, Misty. Yes, I'm back at the resort as you can see. I just need to rest. I'm exhausted. If you don't mind, I'd like to go to my room to lie down." She put her hand to her forehead and rubbed her thumb in small circles around her temple. She looked at me with tired glossy eyes and seemed unsteady holding onto the door for support. She gave me a crooked smile. At that moment, I realized that something was off about her. Another good look at her, and I decided that it was best to back off for the time being.

"Yes, please get some rest. We can talk later, if you want."

"Thank you, Misty. I'll see you when I feel better."

I was not sure if I was doing the right thing, leaving her alone in that condition. She needed her sister to take care of her. "Can I just ask you a couple of quick questions? It'll put my mind at ease."

She sighed loudly. "Sure, go ahead. But make it quick please, I really need to lie down."

"Have you seen your sister yet?"

"Yeah."

"She was extremely worried about you, you know."

"She knows I'm okay, thanks for asking."

"And Scott and Officer Juan? Do they know you're back?"

Julia seemed puzzled at the question at first but recovered quickly. "Yes, they all know." She said while she continued rubbing her temples.

"Sorry, Misty, I really need to rest now. We'll talk later if you don't mind." She turned away from me and entered her room quickly, almost stumbling at the door.

"Ok, let me know if you need anything, Julia," I offered as Julia shut the door behind her.

I stood outside her door not certain that I fully understood what had just happened. Julia was gone for a few days, and no one knew where she was. Yet, she sounded like it was not such a big deal. It could wait until after she was rested, she had told me. How could everyone except me know that she was back and safe? It did not add up. I felt that something strange was going on. The only person who must be in the know was Officer Juan. I texted him in all caps.

PLEASE CALL ME AS SOON AS POSSIBLE! —MISTY .

I pressed send and started pacing up and down the hallway, clenching my phone and willing for a quick reply. A few anxious minutes later I felt a vibration in my hand. The call display read "Officer Juan." I swiped my index finger across the screen in one quick motion.

I tried to temper my voice, but I was not able to curb my excitement, and shouted, "Hello, Officer Juan!"

"Hi, Misty, I just got your text."

"Thanks for getting back to me, Officer Juan. I have just spoken to Julia. She's here, at the resort, in her room right now. Did you know?"

There was a long silent pause at the other end of the line. It was unbearable, and I was about to ask him if he had heard me when he finally spoke.

"Misty, that is great news, indeed! Thank you for letting me know. I've received confirmation that the woman who was discharged from the health centre was indeed Julia. When they admitted her, she said her name was Rose. Rose, is in fact, Julia's middle name. That's why I was not able to make the connection right away. In any event, I will be speaking to her later today. I just haven't had a chance yet. We had an emergency on the island last night. Nothing too serious, but I had to take care of it right away. I'm as relieved as you are, believe me. I will be at the resort in a short while."

"Officer Juan, did you tell Cheryl that you've found her sister?"

"No. I did not know Julia had a sister. Misty, I have to go now. I have an urgent call coming through. Thanks for your help." He ended the call abruptly before I could ask another question.

I stared at my phone thinking that I had two important things to do. First, I needed to talk to

Cheryl to make sure she knew the good news about her sister. I paced up and down the hallway, trying to think of how I could contact her. We had never actually exchanged phone numbers, and I didn't know what room she was in. The few times I'd spoken with her were when we bumped into each other on the beach. And then there was Peter. He would be upset if I went looking for Cheryl without telling him. Reluctantly I decided that my best course of action was to appease Peter and wait for him to wake up. I walked back to the small lounge area in front of our room and sat down, biding my time. I felt like a prisoner in my own mind.

Peter was a wonderful boyfriend, but he could be domineering at times. It all began when I told him that I suffer from chronic anxiety, a condition that has plagued me all my life. His way of caring for me was to try to buffer me from all possible anxiety triggers. But the way he went about it could be suffocating. He needed to be made aware that what he was doing was more detrimental than helpful. It was about time we had a serious talk. But I keep repeating myself. *I've been procrastinating for too long.*

While waiting for Peter to wake up, I was comforted in knowing that Julia was safe, even if she did not look well. Her strained looks could be attributed to the fact that she was tired. What did not seem right to me, was how dismissive she was about the whole matter. She did not even take the time to reassure me about what had really happened to her. As a matter of fact, she made no mention that she nearly drowned. All she said was that Cheryl and Scott were aware of her return. But how could that be? Scott was having drinks with Peter last night. How could he have known that Julia was back? If he did, he would have mentioned it to Peter, and Peter would have most certainly told me. And when I spoke with Officer Juan, he told me something that did not square up. He said that he hadn't yet spoken to Julia. And yet Julia had assured me that everyone knew that she was back. And what about the fact that he didn't even know that Julia had a sister. So many questions, so many suspicions, and no answers that made any real sense.

Enough waiting.

I got up and entered our room to find Peter wide awake sitting on the bed and surfing the internet on his phone.

I sat on the edge of the bed and just stared at him. I could tell he knew I was there sitting next to him, but he made no attempt to acknowledge my presence. This was a pattern with him lately. I was not about to give him the satisfaction to be the one making the first move. I crossed my arms and waited patiently. He would have to acknowledge my presence at some point. And that made me even more determined not to give in. When he finally looked up, I shook my head to signify my displeasure and waited another minute or two before speaking.

"Peter, we need to talk!"

He put his phone down on the nightstand and cleared his throat

"I'm listening."

I stared at him struggling with my thoughts, trying to figure out the best way to give him the news, while worrying about how he might react. After all, Julia was a taboo subject between us. I took more time to consider my options and finally put all caution to the wind and spit out the raw news in one quick breath.

"I saw Julia. She's back…in her room."

There was no reaction from Peter. He just stared blankly at me. It made me feel nervous, but I held on, letting the silence play itself out.

"Wait, what? Are you saying that you saw Julia? Are you sure it's not her sister, Cheryl?

"I spoke to her, Peter. It was Julia."

"When did you talk to her?"

"Just a moment ago. We briefly chatted in front of her room."

"That doesn't make sense, Misty. I thought you went to the rooftop terrace of the resort?"

"Yes, that's where I was going. But on my way there, I passed Julia's room, and I heard a noise down the hall. That's when I saw Julia about to enter her room. You can imagine my surprise."

Peter kept staring blankly at me, then at the ceiling. He was quiet. I thought he would have more questions, and his silence really annoyed me.

"Well…aren't you going to say you're relieved to hear that Julia is safe?"

I could tell Peter didn't like my tone, and he responded in kind, "Of course I'm relieved to hear that she's not harmed!"

I swallowed hard and tried to better control my emotions. "Sorry, Peter, it's a lot to take in, I know. I'm as confused as you are now and happy for her at the same time."

Peter finally relented. "You're right, Misty. It's great news."

I was relieved. At long last Peter was seeing it my way.

"Peter, when you were with Scott last night, did he mention to you anything about Julia? Did he tell you if he had heard from her?"

"It's funny you should ask. I was just thinking about Scott too. He's going to be very happy that Julia has returned. But I don't think he knows."

"That's strange. Julia just told me that Scott knew that she was back."

"Maybe she called him when he went back to his room?"

"That's possible, I guess."

"I have Scott's number, let me ask him right now." Peter grabbed his phone from the nightstand. He seemed edgy, which was unusual for him.

"Hey buddy, it's Peter…sorry if I woke you up." He listened to Scott for a second or two, then said. "Hey, did you know Julia's back at the resort? Yeah, she's in her room now."

I could hear Scott's muffled voice, but I couldn't make out what he was saying to Peter.

"Yes, I know, it's great news. Misty spoke with her a few minutes ago…Yes, she seemed okay according to Misty…So, you had no idea about her being back at the resort?"

Peter looked at me and shook his head.

"Apparently, Julia told Misty that you already knew. That's weird, I know." I heard Peter tell Scott. His expression changed as he turned to face me. "...Just a second, let me ask her... Scott wants to go to Julia's room to see if she needs anything. Do you think it's a good idea?"

I took a moment to think about it. "Yes, tell Scott it's a good idea but not right now. I just spoke to her, and she said she was tired and needed to lie down for a bit."

Peter relayed the message and waited for Scott's response. He nodded several times and then said, "Okay, bud, let's do lunch at say, noon-ish. See you at the beach bar restaurant. Ciao."

"So, Scott had no idea about what's going on with Julia?"

"He didn't have a clue, but as you can imagine, he's happy and relieved to hear that she's okay. Why do you think Julia told you that he already knew she'd returned?"

"I don't know, but she seemed very tired, almost distressed... Something was definitely off about her."

"What makes you say that?"

"She kept rubbing her temples, and her eyes were like glass when she looked at me. She seemed unsteady on her feet, and couldn't wait to get into her room."

Peter stared at me stone-faced. I could not tell if he was intrigued or in deep thought.

"Peter?"

"What?"

"What are you thinking about?"

"This whole thing about Julia's disappearance and then reappearing out of nowhere sounds fishy to me, don't you think?"

"Do you think she is on drugs?"

Now Peter was definitely intrigued.

"I really don't know what to make of it."

Peter looked pensive and kept rubbing his chin. I knew that was the way he processed thorny issues. He was a results-driven problem solver who would not let go until he got to the bottom of the issue. He could be obsessive about it. All the reason why his sudden change of subject took me by total surprise.

"Hey sweetheart, do you realize this is our last full day here?"

"Yes, I know."

"Well, let's not waste our last day in Roatan! Let's get out of here and enjoy the day to the fullest, okay?" Peter put his arms around my waist and squeezed me hard. I felt a huge sense of relief. Julia had returned, and like Peter, I desperately wanted to put the whole saga behind me. I allowed myself to melt into his arms. He kissed me on the mouth, stroked my hair gently, and murmured the words I was longing to hear.

"I love you, Misty."

"You're such a sweetie, Peter."

He held my face in his hands and kissed me once again. All seemed so perfect.

"Hey, Peter, why don't we head up to the terrace and have our breakfast over there?"

"That's a wonderful idea, honey."

We took a few minutes to freshen up. Then we walked hand in hand through the gardens. It was pleasantly warm, and a gentle ocean breeze brushed our faces. Another typical beautiful morning in Roatan, which somehow felt extra special this day. The glowing sun above the azure ocean, and the subtle perfume of the rose gardens made our second-last morning in Roatan feel almost magical.

We grabbed our seats at our usual table on the terrace overlooking the glistening ocean. We kept quiet for the most part. I thought about how important Peter was to me. I made myself a promise to never hold back anything from him again. No more half-truths, no more lies, total honesty was paramount. Peter's bursts of anger were something he alone had to work on and learn to control. And I made a resolution to speak up when I felt that his behavior was not acceptable.

Peter rested his left arm on the table and took a long look at me. I immediately recognized the shift in his body language as a sign that he wanted to tell me something important. He rubbed his chin a couple of times, seemingly struggling with what he was about to tell me.

"You know, Misty, you had me scared. Things between us were so bad that I was sure you were about to dump me."

"Really? What made you think that?" I nudged him.

He then took a deep breath before finally answering me.

"Several times during our trip, I was convinced that I was going to lose you. You've been so anxious and stressed ever since Julia went missing. I understand you were concerned but you really were not yourself...And I promised..." Peter stopped mid-sentence and looked away.

I pressed him to tell me more. "And you promised what?"

Peter looked me in the eyes. "Trust me about what I'm about to tell you. I did not go behind your back. Before leaving, your mother made me promise that I would take care of you and to make sure you were relaxed on this vacation. Your mom and sister have been so worried about you lately because you've been so stressed at work. You really needed this break. But when you began to obsess about Julia, a woman you had only just met, I didn't know what to do. This vacation was supposed to be a relaxing break from everything that was stressing you at work. And I'm afraid it has done the opposite."

He paused one more time to test my reaction. I waited patiently for him to continue.

"...and I'm sorry I've been tough with you at times. I didn't handle it very well, I know. I ended up upsetting you more instead. It was wrong of me. I should have taken the time to calmly explain to you where I was coming from. Misty, I've told you so many times that I think you worry about other people far too much. You need to take care of yourself first before you take care of others. I mean, you were so consumed with Julia, to the point of making yourself sick."

"You're so right, Peter. I haven't been myself. I really regret forgetting to bring my medication on this trip. I should have told you right away. I'm so sorry about that. But you know, I can't stop caring for others. It's my nature. There's nothing you or I can do about it. My anxiety disorder is another matter. Sometimes I just cannot control it. I know that. I really try hard with meditation and deep breathing exercises, which do help somewhat. But this time, on this trip, what I really needed was your understanding.

I was deeply disturbed by what was going on with Julia. And to be completely honest with you, I felt like you weren't always there for me."

"I'm so sorry, Misty, I'll try harder to be more understanding from now on. I know I mishandled the whole situation. You had every right to be angry at me. And you are right to point it out to me. We'll be home tomorrow night, and I'll work hard to make sure it doesn't happen again. It'll be fine. I'll be more patient. I'll take care of you, I promise."

I was so relieved to hear those words, *I'll take care of you.*

I wanted to be taken care of.

I needed to be taken care of.

"Thank you, my sweetheart. You've no idea how much that means to me."

Once the air had been cleared between us, I felt the aching need to reassess my feelings towards Peter. I knew where he stood. He was truly in love with me, even if sometimes he had a peculiar way of showing it. His intentions were always noble. That much I knew. As far as I was concerned, the best answer I could come out with was that I cared dearly about him. The rest, I was afraid, was very much a work in progress.

My father always told me to let time do its work when I was not sure of myself. Some wise advice that has served me well with many difficult decisions. But what if I could speed up time? Everything would be so clear to me in an instant. There would be no room for self-doubt. No need for procrastination. No need for false hope. Just a simple unbridled truth. An impossible dream, sadly. At the very least, Peter deserved more clarity on my part. He should not have to wait a long time

After our heart-to-heart conversation, we had a long and enjoyable time together. We had resolved some issues. There was no need to talk anymore about it. We just felt good being in each other's company. *God, I hope it lasts.*

There was precious little time left in our vacation in Roatan, and we were both eager to make sure that our recollections of our last moments on this island were truly memorable. It felt as if our whole future together hinged on how successful this day will turn out to be. Breakfast was a cathartic experience, and then we went back to our room to change into our bathing suits and grab our towels. Not a word was exchanged between us all this time for fear of spoiling the wonderful spell that enveloped us. I reached for my phone and my novel which were on the nightstand. Once again, I hesitated whether I should take the phone with me or leave it behind. That issue seemed to be a constant dilemma with me since I had landed on this island. I took a peek at Peter and realized he had been watching me all this time. Peter grinned and shook his head while holding onto his own phone.

"Oh, I see, you approve of me leaving my phone behind, but you're bringing your phone to the pool," I said teasingly.

"Sweetie, you know I need to keep up with my hockey team! It's the playoffs!" He laughed out loud.

"Hon, I wouldn't dream of keeping you away from your team!"

"At last, we agree on something!" We both laughed like a happy couple once again.

We found two lounge chairs under an umbrella by the pool. I went for a short swim, towelled off, and picked up my book. Peter had not moved an inch from his chair, consumed with his phone as usual. I read my novel for a little while when nature called.

"Darling, I'll be right back, I'm heading to our room to use the washroom."

"Okay," said Peter without looking up from his phone.

I was about to enter my room, when I spotted Julia walking briskly down the hall. I called out her name twice. She slowed down but did not stop. When I reached her, I noticed that she had put on makeup and fixed her hair in a bun. She looked radiant.

"I'm glad, I caught up with you. How are you?"

"I'm fine."

"I'm so happy to hear that you feel better. You look great by the way. Do you think we can talk now about what happened to you?"

It took her a few beats to answer. "I'm sorry, Misty, but I'm in a hurry. I'm already late for an appointment at the police station. I have to complete the filing of my deposition, or they will not allow me to leave the island."

I watched her leave in total disbelief. She had once again found an excuse to avoid answering my question.

I took a quick peek back down the hallway and by coincidence, Officer Juan was coming around the corner, heading for Julia's room, with a file in his hand. This was my opportunity to clarify a few things concerning Julia, and I did not hesitate to take it.

"Hello, Officer Juan."

"Oh, hi, Misty. How are you doing today?"

"I'm fine, thanks. Is everything okay, officer?"

"Yes, why are you asking?

"Oh, nothing much. It's just that Julia told me a few minutes ago that she had to go to the police station to file some sort of paperwork."

"That's strange. I'm pretty sure that I told her that I'll be meeting her at the resort to finalize her statement. I guess I better get back to the station and catch her before she leaves Roatan tomorrow."

"Oh, yeah, so are we. We were on the same flight coming here too."

"Misty, now that I've got you here, I need to ask you something that's been bothering me about this case."

His words struck warning bells in my head. "What is it, officer?" I said nervously.

"It's about her friend."

"What about her friend?"

"Well, that's just it. She told Miguel that she was meeting her friend when he dropped her off at Little French Key. Where was her friend when she nearly drowned? I asked the kids who rescued her if they had seen anyone with her.

They told me that she was alone. Do you know anything about this friend?"

"Nothing other than what you just told me. Do you think that she lied about meeting a friend?"

The police officer stared at me shaking his head. "I don't know what is going on with her. Why make up a story about a fictitious friend? It's beyond me."

"Did you ask her who the friend she was supposedly meeting at Little French Key?

"No luck there either. Julia refused to answer me when I asked. In my opinion, Julia is either a reckless thrill seeker, or she was looking for trouble…if you know what I mean?"

"What are you saying? Do you think she intentionally wanted to drown?"

"Maybe. That could be what happened. The water taxi driver, Miguel, did indeed give Julia a ride to Little French Key that night. According to some witnesses, she went for a swim and was caught by the strong underwater current in an area that is off- limits. Luckily for her a bunch of local kids fooling around on the beach saw her enter the water. They told me that they yelled at her to get out of the water, that it was too dangerous, but she ignored them. Before long they saw her struggling in the water fighting against the strong current. She was about to drown when they caught up with her and brought her back to shore unconscious. It all happened just the way Miguel told us."

I gasped. "Wow, thank God they were there! They saved her life! I just don't understand what she was thinking by going there so late at night in the first place. Why Little French Key? If she wanted to swim, she could have stayed at the resort."

Officer Juan looked perplexed. "I don't understand it either. But Little French Key is a very popular place. Maybe she heard about it and wanted to see it for herself. What happened to Julia reminds me of an incident that took place many years ago. I was a rookie cop at the time and, early one morning, I got a distress call coming from Little French Key. I rushed to the scene to find a young man sobbing on the beach over the lifeless body of his wife. I will never forget what he said to me. It seemed so off. He kept repeating, 'Oh my God…Oh my God. I don't understand, this can't be happening, my wife is a good swimmer. I tried to rescue her, but the current was too strong. Oh my God.' And he kept sobbing. I couldn't get another word out of him. Later on, that day, I found out that he and his late wife were indeed experienced divers and swimmers. They had snorkelled and dove all over the world. But the way the husband was acting seemed a bit odd to me. He seemed so defensive, wanting to avoid any blame. I shared my concerns with my captain, who told me there was nothing there. I didn't know any better, so I filed the case as an accident as I was instructed by my superior."

I had goosebumps hearing the story. It could have happened to Julia.

"Sorry, Misty, I know it's a sad story, but it just goes to show you how strong the currents are in that area. Even the best swimmers don't stand a chance. Julia should have known. There are signs everywhere warning about the danger. She is very lucky to be alive."

I shook my head in disbelief. "And what about Cheryl?"

"What about Cheryl? Who is Cheryl?"

"Her sister. Didn't she tell you about her?"

"I've no idea who you are talking about. Julia never mentioned to me that she had a sister."

"But Cheryl told us that she got a call from the Roatan police informing her that her sister went missing. She said that she talked to someone at the police station. I assume it was you. Did you not talk to her?"

"That's news to me, Misty. I can assure you no one at the station has called or talked to Cheryl. I'd have known about it as I'm the officer in charge of the investigation."

"But how can that be? I spoke to her several times, and so did Peter and Scott. She was so worried about Julia. That's why she came to the island."

"Misty, I don't know what to tell you. Lots of people come and go to Roatan. I can't give you a better explanation."

"But don't you think that's weird, Officer Juan?"

"It sounds to me that Julia is a very private person. In any event, Julia has been found, and she is safe and sound, and I better get going if I want to catch her to get her full deposition. There's nothing I can do about Cheryl.'"

Officer Juan saw the distress on my face and tried to reassure me. "Listen, Misty, this case is closed as far as I'm concerned. There's no longer any missing person. Julia is unharmed, and hopefully she's learned her lesson. You've been very helpful, and I thank you for that. But I think you need to forget the whole thing and try to enjoy your last day on the island. I am so sorry this all happened while you were here on your vacation."

"Perhaps I was meant to be here?"

"Perhaps you were. This island is a mystical place." He smiled at me and then checked his watch. "Sorry, Misty. I really have to run. Have a safe trip home. I hope you'll come back to visit Roatan again."

"Thank you, officer," I said.

Officer Juan nodded and walked away. I stood in the hallway, staring at the empty space ahead of me for quite a long time. The whole thing about Julia was really nagging me. What Officer Juan had told me seemed like a story half told. There were simply too many gaps. I was anxious to tell Peter what I'd just learned, so I quickly made my way back to the pool area. Peter was still on the chaise playing with his phone. This time I kicked the leg of the chair to get his attention.

"Peter, I need to talk to you."

"Just a second, let me finish reading this article, I'll be with you in a second."

"It's important, Peter."

He put his phone down, looked at me, and sighed. "What is it, Misty?"

"I just spoke to Officer Juan. He just came from Julia's room. He told me that all is well with her."

Peter squinted his eyes. "We already knew that, Misty. Is something else bothering you? What is it this time?"

"Well, Julia didn't look that well to me when I saw her yesterday. Also, Officer Juan told me something about her sister that really troubles me."

"What about Cheryl?"

"He said he never heard of Cheryl. Did not know that Julia had a sister. Never spoke to her. Never told her that her sister was missing. Had no idea that Cheryl was in Roatan."

"Huh? What's he talking about? We all saw Cheryl at the resort and spoke to her!"

"I know, it's strange. But what is even weirder is that he thinks Julia lied about meeting a friend at Little French Key."

"So, what do you think is going on? Where is Cheryl now?"

"I don't know. The whole thing is so bizarre. Only Julia would know where she is. Someone needs to talk to her asap."

"Misty, there has to be a logical explanation." Peter, the ever rational analyst, sensed my anxiety level and tried to calm me down. "We can't let this whole matter consume us. I mean, it sounds odd I agree with you, but we know Julia is safe, and I'm sure Cheryl is too. That's all that really matters. We're all going home tomorrow. This whole thing will be forgotten. Let's just enjoy our last day before we go back to the freezing cold back home."

Peter reached out to me and held me tightly in his arms. It felt good and secure but not entirely satisfying.

I can't let this rest.

CHAPTER 16

*"If you want to conquer the anxiety of life,
live the moment, live in the breath."*

—Amit Ray

$\mathcal{S}$omething felt different about our last day in Roatan. Our vacation was nearly over. Soon we would be home with lots of memories and a suntan. It was not so long ago that Peter and I had some major disagreements. But that was in the past now. We had found our peace. Julia was still on my mind, even though I knew she was back and safe. But for the time being, I thought it best to let it rest.

Peter picked Roatan looking for a place where everything would be so perfect that its magic would rub on us. He chose well. Roatan had given us another chance at serenity. Indeed, a fairy-tale island with plentiful sun, sea, and sand was the perfect recipe to restore a couple's happiness. In our case, it just took some time to sink in.

We spent the day lounging by the pool, soaking in every last ounce of sunshine. I was able to keep any lingering anxiety in check by swimming and taking a long walk along the beach. I knew I would feel better once I was back on my medication. I just had to be patient.

Reflecting on my life made me wonder what I would have done if I had not met Peter. Our timing was less than ideal as we both carried the heavy baggage of recently failed relationships. Yet, we clicked. For sure it took a while, largely due to my insecurities but in the end, we managed to make a go of it.

I was blessed with a good and caring upbringing, but it was not perfect. Both my parents loved me dearly. They were good providers and always gave me enough support to let me make important decisions on my own. The problem was that I was shy and reserved and it took me forever to make up my mind. As I grew older my indecisiveness became even worse. I used to find every excuse in the book to avoid making a decision. Procrastination was my middle name.

In retrospect I wished that my anxiety disorder had been addressed earlier on by my parents. It was above all the root cause of my lack of confidence. I sought to avoid stressful situations like the plague, and the whole critical process of decision making only served to feed my anxiety. Unfortunately, my parents were the product of an older generation, where mental health issues were a taboo subject, not to be spoken of, least of all acknowledged. My mother's own mental health did not help my cause, either.

When Peter came into my life, it felt like a breath of fresh air. He was not only my boyfriend, he was also my saviour, in a very unusual sense. In so many ways through push and shove, he helped me confront my fears. He made me realize that my condition was not something to be embarrassed about. He was able to accomplish this major shift in how I approached my anxiety disorder that no therapists were able to do. And there were several of them. They mostly focused the therapy sessions on breathing techniques and medications. And when they tried behaviour change therapy, I put up a wall and resisted any attempt to let them in my mind. I just could not deal with it and walked away to another therapist. I was wrong, of course. What was needed all along was the will to get better, the desire to confront head on the overpowering emotions that had taken over my mind, and to let them go.

"No one is perfect, I love you the way you are," Peter once told me.

His words struck a chord in me. Peter helped me recognize that what I had been doing all along, was not working. I could not hold onto relationships, always being afraid that my secret would be uncovered somehow. He made me become aware of my fear, thereby enabling me to work on the emotional rollercoaster that consumed me in moments of crises.

Later on, that evening, while I was drying my hair, I heard Peter speaking on the phone. All I could manage to hear were a few dribs and drabs here and there.

"…okay buddy, see you later, take care. Bye."

"Who was that, Peter?" I asked as I stepped out of the washroom.

"Scott."

"Oh? What were you guys talking about?"

"Julia."

"Please, don't tease me, Peter. Just tell me what he said."

"He went to see Julia in her room this afternoon. He told me that she seemed fine. In fact, he had a long talk with her. He asked her to join him for dinner at the beach restaurant, but she declined. She wanted to pack or used some other lame excuse like that."

"Well that's good to hear, I mean that she's fine."

"Yeah, of course."

"Did she say anything about what happened at Little French Key?"

"No. That's what's strange. Scott said that she quickly changed the subject when he broached the drowning accident."

"It must have been such a traumatic experience. She probably can't talk about it yet."

Peter nodded in agreement. "I guess so. But get this! Scott told me that out of the blue she had a change of heart and agreed to have dinner with him as long as they would eat in her room."

"What's so strange about that, after all she's been through? The girl wants to take it easy. I understand that. By the way, did she say anything about her sister?"

"Yes, apparently Cheryl went home already."

"Huh? Why wouldn't she accompany Julia home?"

"I don't know. She told Scott that her sister had to get home as soon as possible. She didn't elaborate."

"You know, Peter, it still baffles me that Officer Juan didn't have a clue about Cheryl. It's a small island. People just don't show up like that and no one notices them!"

"You're right. Maybe Officer Juan is not very good at his job," Peter said with a smirk. "He didn't seem to put much effort into it. Or maybe… never mind. Hey, Misty, you know what?"

"What is it, sweetheart?"

"You look amazing!" Peter took me in his arms and kissed me. I melted into his arms.

"Thanks, hon. This feels really good," I said as I held onto him tightly and passionately kissed him back, reminiscent of our very first kiss.

"I love you," I whispered into his ear.

He pulled away slightly and stared at me with his beautiful blue eyes. "I love you too."

Peter and I decided to have our last dinner in Roatan on the beach. It would be a fitting end to a vacation that had brought us so many surprises—some good and some bad. I'd read on the resort bulletin board that there'd be a candlelight dinner with musical accompaniment at the beach bar restaurant that night. That's where we were heading hand in hand. Peter looked particularly handsome in his white shirt, which contrasted beautifully with his deep suntan. The night was young, and I felt relatively free of worries. A wonderful feeling I'd missed for too long.

The restaurant was already half full of patrons when we arrived. We were seated at a table close to the live music stand, which pleased me greatly. A few yards away, the ocean waves were making their last retreat of the evening, perhaps their way of wishing us farewell. The night was set for a magical send-off.

Once back home, we would certainly reminisce about our time in Roatan. I wondered what memories Peter would carry with him. As for me, it was a journey that tested me in so many ways. Had I been successful in overcoming my angst? Only time would tell. For now, I was in the mood for a celebration with my lover.

"Peter, darling, thank you so much for being here and sharing this with me." I made a dramatic arch motion with my arms in the air around me. "All of this."

Peter became emotional. I'd not seen him like that for a long time. I fought back tears and kissed him. A beautiful evening was about to unfold indeed.

While sipping our cocktails, I glanced at the bar and saw the jolly bartender preparing drinks and chatting away with guests. He was such a happy fellow. I couldn't help but smile at him when he caught me watching him. He held up a glass, and I lifted my cocktail glass, mouthing, "*Cheers.*"

Peter ordered the catch of the day with herbed vegetables as his main course. I chose the truffle risotto, which was cooked to perfection, and I savoured every bite. Once dessert was served, the singer walked on the stage and introduced herself. She turned out to be the same singer from Vintage Pearl.

"Hey, Peter, look who it is," I whispered, and he nodded recognizing her.

She opened her act with a song about Roatan. It brought me back to the wonderful evening Peter had arranged for us. It was not that long ago, and yet so many things had happened since then. I let the music carry me away to that wonderful birthday night spent with Peter when everything seemed so perfect.

On stage, the singer intoned a couple more tunes accompanied by her acoustic guitar. Then she announced she would take requests from guests. Scott was the first one to walk over to the stage. He whispered something to the singer, who smiled up at him. Peter and I looked at each other, wondering what Scott was up to. I knew that Julia could not be very far. I was not wrong. She was sitting at a table off to the side. She was wearing a beautiful white dress and had her hair done up, which accentuated her exotic looks. Meanwhile Scott had spotted us and was making his way to our table.

"Hey lovebirds, did you enjoy your dinner?"

"Yeah, bud, it was delicious. What about you and Julia?"

"It was kind of peaceful eating in her room. I managed to convince her to come here after our dinner to listen to the music. I just requested a song for her. I should really get back to our table," he said as he looked in Julia's direction. "I'll catch up with you guys tomorrow. Have a great evening."

The singer opened her second act with a dedication from Scott to a "special young lady." And she started singing, in her melodious voice, *The Rose* by Amanda McBroom and made famous by Bette Midler.

It was a song I knew well. The second stanza in particular spoke to me in a very special way. I always had a strong emotional connection to this song from the very first time I heard it on the radio. I could not explain it. Something about the lyrics, or maybe the melody had something to do with it, or possibly the sadness in the singer's voice had found a way to touch my heart and brought tears to my eyes every time.

Of all the beautiful songs in the world, why did the singer choose this one to entertain us on our last night in Roatan? Could it be a mere coincidence, the draw of a random selection, perhaps? The time, place, and circumstances in which the song took place, however, compelled me to think of another possibility. What if some mystical force was at work, and a message from the heart had been sent my way?

I looked at Peter as he reached for my hand. I became very emotional listening to "The Rose," and I could barely fight back tears, which by now were starting to roll freely down my cheeks. I excused myself and rushed to the restroom. Hiding behind a closed stall door, I could no longer hold back, and I began to sob uncontrollably. Alone, leaning against the door, I kept on weeping, crying, and sobbing for a very long time. I was thankful no one else had entered the washroom. I was not just sad, I was hurting. The song had triggered memories that I thought had been buried forever. Yet the tears somehow felt cathartic.

I heard someone open the door of the washroom and use the sink. I tried to keep quiet and wiped my tears with a tissue. I needed to pull myself together and get back to Peter. I waited until the woman left the washroom to rinse my face with cold water and fixed my makeup. I was grateful it was dark outside, so the redness in my face would not be too obvious.

Peter was sitting where I had left him at our table. He looked up when he noticed me walking back from the restroom.

"Sweetheart, what's wrong?" he whispered in my ear as another love melody was playing in the background.

"All is well, Peter. Please don't worry, I just needed a moment to myself. It really hit me how the whole ordeal with Julia had come between us. And the song, 'The Rose,' reminded me how lucky we are, my love."

Even in the darkness, Peter could tell I had been crying. He didn't press me to explain myself further. He just held my hand tightly and sat close to me for the rest of the evening.

The next morning, Peter and I woke up early in order to pack before leaving for our flight back home. It was another beautiful day in Roatan. We had both slept well and woke up without the heavy burdens of the previous days. Nothing to stress us, just the kind of morning the website of the resort had advertised.

Scott walked by as we were sipping our coffee on the terrace and waved at us. Peter gave him a thumbs up and Scott took it as an invitation to join us.

"Hey, you guys," Scott said as he sat down grinning ear to ear.

"Hey, buddy, how are you doing? Are you all packed?"

"Yup, I checked out already and my bags are in the lobby with the concierge. Time to say goodbye to this lovely, little piece of nirvana."

"Back to reality, eh," I said glumly and then added with a playful smile, "So, Scott, how was your evening with Julia? Please tell us."

"It went well. All is good…pretty, pretty good."

"Come on, Scott, stop kidding around. Tell us at least that you didn't make her cry this time?"

"Well, if you absolutely have to know, she seems to have somewhat recovered from her ordeal. And no, I did not make her cry. But she was very quiet throughout the evening. A word here, a word there, nothing substantive though. Look, I don't mean to be insensitive about what happened to her, but it's a weird way to make a guy feel like his company is appreciated. Anyway, she told me that her father will be meeting her at the airport."

"Well, that's good, that she won't go home alone."

Scott shrugged. "I guess so."

"So, what is it, Scott?" I said, sensing that there was more Scott wanted to tell us.

"Spill it out man," Peter pressed.

"Well, as the night went on, she gave me some sort of an explanation as to why she can be difficult at times, especially when she is around people. When she clamps up for instance–the way she treats me sometimes."

"Don't feel sorry for yourself, Scott. The poor girl nearly drowned. Cut her some slack!"

"That's not it, guys. She told me that she's still haunted by the passing of her mother when she was young."

"Poor thing. What exactly happened to her mother?" I asked.

"She drowned while scuba diving or snorkeling. I'm not exactly sure how it happened."

"Oh my God! How awful! Cheryl had told me that they had lost their mother, but she never told me how it happened."

Scott glanced at Peter and paused for a moment before making eye contact with me, as if wanting Peter's approval to tell me more.

"Get this, her mother drowned here in Roatan. Talk about a coincidence!"

I took one quick look at Peter and instantly knew what he was thinking. I felt a chill run through my body as the old article on the internet flashed through my mind.

"What do you mean, here in Roatan? At this resort?" Peter asked.

"No, at Little French Key. She told me that she was there when it happened. She was standing on the beach when her father came out of the water screaming for help. She saw everything. She saw the body of her mother being pulled from the water, and her father trying to revive her by doing CPR. It was too late, she had swallowed too much water. She heard her father scream his lungs out. Everyone was frantic around her. No one paid any attention to her. She told me that she felt totally helpless, not really grasping what was going on."

"Poor thing, did she tell you if Cheryl was with her when it happened?"

"No. She didn't mention anything about her sister, and I didn't think of asking her."

I choked in tears. "How awful it must have been to witness the tragic death of her own mother at such a young age. I could not imagine how I would have reacted if something like that had happened to me." I covered my face with my hands. When I removed them moments later, tears were still rolling down my cheeks.

"Misty, hon, are you okay?" Peter asked, seeing the pain on my face.

I gave him a silent nod, hiding my grief deep inside of me. *How does someone recover from such a tragedy?*

"Sorry, guys, I wasn't sure how much I should tell you. I didn't want to upset you, but I thought you would want to know, to help you understand her."

"It's okay, buddy. Thank you for sharing. It's good that you told us," Peter quickly interjected.

"Yes, thank you, Scott. You did the right thing by telling us," I said, echoing Peter's response.

Peter turned to me. He could see how deeply affected I was by what Scott had told us. He tried his best to comfort and reassure me in his own way. "Sweetheart, all is well now. Julia is safe, and she's going home and her father will pick her up at the airport."

I desperately wanted to agree with him. If Julia felt the need to tell Scott, it was probably because she thought that it might help him better understand her. I prayed that she did not misplace her confidence in him.

Scott had related the whole tragic incident about Julia's mother's drowning in the same even tone he employed most of the time. I watched him as he walked away, wondering how he was able to show so little emotion. Whatever he was hiding inside, he hid it well. Scott was not unique. I've met and unfortunately dealt with this type of man many times in my life. Accustomed to having their own way, thanks to their good looks and wits, they did not easily accept rejection. How they might react to being turned down did not differ very much from one to the other. Resorting to anger was usually the norm at the beginning. And when the realization hits that anger did not solve anything, they revert to diminishing the importance of the person who rejected them. In the case of Scott, I saw only the first half of the reaction. It seemed to me that he never lost his interest in Julia. His infatuation for her seemed real. His problem was that he had a hard time coming to terms with his feelings. *Maybe that's the secret to a carefree life*, I thought, then quickly discarded the whole idea as pure nonsense. I turned my attention to Peter and asked him to join me for a last walk along the beach before grabbing the bus back to the airport.

"We don't have much time, Misty. Why don't you go ahead, and I'll bring our luggage to the lobby and check us out."

I gave Peter a peck on the cheek, and we left the restaurant together. We walked along the narrow pathway and parted ways in front of the main lobby.

"I'll meet you in the reception area in twenty minutes," I said as I began to make my way towards the beach.

I walked slowly, making the most of my last precious moments in Roatan, taking as many mental pictures as I could to bring with me back home. I took off my sandals and walked on the wet sand alongside the shoreline. The water was warm and soothing and so inviting. I stopped to gaze at the ocean and my surroundings while taking several deep breaths. At a distance, the beach vendors were roaming the grounds of the resort looking for tourists who might have shown the slightest interest in their trinkets. Over on my right, the docks were swarming with fishermen busy folding their nets and getting their boats ready for their next fishing expedition. Nearby, a large group of fresh arrivals had gathered around the beach bar. Most were wearing long sleeve sweaters and were struggling to hold onto their heavy coats. They looked like an excited happy bunch who had just landed on the island, hardly believing their good luck.

How much and for how long will the memories of Roatan remain etched in my mind, I wondered? But at this point, my most pressing question was whether my stay on this wonderful island had achieved its purpose. Coming here was an experiment to test the strength of our relationship. In some ways, the island had done its work. Rough edges between us had been exposed and hammered out. Now would come the hard work to smooth things out and to hopefully find a happy compromise to live by—a daunting task for sure but not an impossible one.

There were times when I felt that nothing would help. I'd been vacationing in an absolute paradise where everything seemed to move along the rhythm of the ocean waves—majestic, repetitive, and enduring. Always moving forward, leaving behind any turmoil beneath the surface, only to find a final resting place on the shore. It seemed to me that the inhabitants of Roatan understood the real meaning of life. All they had to do was to look to the ocean for inspiration and realize that one must not dwell too long on the past and focus instead on the present and what's ahead in order to ascend to a peaceful state of mind.

In so many ways I should consider myself to be very lucky. Yet, I seemed to never be able to fully appreciate the precious moments that life has given me, time and time again. My anxiety disorder has always been a major impediment, a barrier that I was never able to fully overcome. I always felt that a curse had been thrown my way. But was that a fair assessment? What if my mental condition was a self-inflicted wound, a trick of the mind designed to mask my insecurities?

Peter was right after all. I needed to find a way to let go of my fears. This trip to Roatan was more than just a means to find out if we were truly compatible. It had another purpose that was kept hidden from me until now. I had to get away from all that was troubling me at work, the daily grind, the stressful environment, and above all, the dire pessimism that permeated all around me. That much I understood. But underneath it all, I needed to resolve the root cause of my mental disorder if I wanted to live a full and fruitful life.

The last leg of a wave reached my feet, reminding me that all was not lost. More was to come if only I could stand still and allow the source of my pain wash away from the deep recess of my mind. Roatan would show me the way. All I had to do was to let it happen and half the battle would have been won. But what if I couldn't make it work? What if my mind would not cooperate? There was so much I needed to resolve on my own.

I'd hoped the walk would help calm me, but Julia had a way of creeping into my mind. I thought about the tragic death of her mother and how it must have affected her. I remembered the way she seemed to zone out at times and how she wanted to be left alone. I could not forget how Cheryl had described her sister, Julia, as the strong one. The one who would read her stories when their father was away on his business trips. And I recalled, and could never forget, how anxious I felt this past week. Julia's disappearance had deeply troubled me. I recognized that it was time to go home and get back to my daily routine and not to forget my anxiety medication ever again.

I said a silent goodbye to the ocean and put on my sandals. I walked towards the lobby and stopped at a restroom along the way. I needed to freshen up before boarding the airport bus. I thought I was alone in the bathroom until I heard a toilet flush, and a woman came out of the stall to use the sink beside me. It was Julia. Our paths had crossed once again. I looked at her and felt an unmistakable sense that this was not a mere coincidence. A mystical force had brought us together at this very moment. But what was the reason? What purpose did it serve? I could see in Julia's eyes that she'd also sensed something unusual happening between us. We stood apart staring at each other for a couple of minutes.

I broke the spell and chimed, "Oh, Julia, I'm so glad I bumped into you. I'd have hated myself if I did not give you a proper goodbye and a big hug. I do hope that you're feeling better."

Julia tried to smile at me, but I could see that it did not come easily. So, we simply hugged each other, not wanting to let go.

"I'm okay, thank you. I just need to get home," she finally said while still holding onto me.

"Listen Julia, if you ever need to talk to someone, please don't hesitate to give me a call."

"Misty, that's really kind of you, but you don't even know me. And I'm quite a handful, you know."

"I'm a handful too, we'll get along just fine," I said, really meaning it.

"You? No way, I don't believe you."

"Just ask Peter! He'll tell you!"

It was a terrible joke, I knew it. But it worked, and we both started laughing.

"Seriously though, I would like to keep in touch with you."

"Really? Thank you, I'd like that too, Misty. I promise you I'll tell you everything you want to know, when I get home.

"You mean it?"

"Absolutely."

We exchanged numbers and walked together to the main lobby. It was time to board the shuttle bus that would take us to the airport. Peter spotted us and motioned me to follow him. Not far behind were Scott and Julia, who boarded the bus together. Peter and I didn't chat much during the ride and neither did Julia and Scott. Some rowdy girls sitting at the back of the bus kept the ride lively with laughter. I wondered if they were the same girls on the plane with us when we first arrived in Roatan.

Were they even aware of what had happened on the island?

CHAPTER 17

With stress comes anxiety. With anxiety comes worries and fear. Happy thoughts bring happiness.

We arrived at Roatan's minuscule airport. After we checked in, there was some time to relax in the waiting area. I told Peter that I wanted to stretch my legs. I took a walk around the little terminal and spotted a large guest book folded open on a pedestal. The sign above it read: "The department of tourism would greatly appreciate your help to improve the experience of visitors by sharing your thoughts about Roatan." I flipped through a few pages and read some of the inscriptions. They were very complimentary for the most part. Someone had lost their favorite hat and was very upset about that, but most visitors were very pleased with their stay in Roatan. *What could I write? I love this tiny island, the people and the landscape, the remoteness and the warm hospitality…but did my time here serve me well? Was it helpful to me? I had needed this vacation so badly. But I had been troubled by so many turns of events. Julia had almost drowned, and I had had many disagreements with Peter. My stay in Roatan had been a struggle, I must confess. But in the end, Peter and I had found a way to resolve our differences. Or so I hope.*

I decided to focus on the positive as my parents had taught me. I simply wrote, *Thank you, Roatan. Stay beautiful.* I then drew a heart and a maple leaf. My father loved to travel, and I knew he would have wanted me to be on this vacation despite everything. He taught me to look for the silver lining when things don't go exactly as I wish. *"You can always learn from your failures and do things better next time."* I remembered his words fondly and gave them some thought. I vowed to never give into my anxiety again and to live by one principle—be honest with those you love.

Our flight number was announced, and Peter came to get me. We took our place in line for boarding. Julia Rose and Scott were just ahead of us.

Julia Rose…what a truly beautiful name.

The flight back to Toronto was uneventful. Most of the passengers fell asleep, likely because they were too tired, had too much to drink, or simply had too much fun at the resort before takeoff. As for me, I was dozing most of the time as it was the only way for me to survive the flight without a panic attack.

I woke up feeling Peter gently tugging on my shoulder. He knew I was nervous about landing. He held my arm and whispered, "Everything is going to be okay."

I smiled back at him but held onto his arm tightly for reassurance.

The plane landed smoothly on the tarmac, and the passengers applauded the pilot.

Meanwhile, the flight attendants were busy getting the aircraft ready for debarkation. I felt good being back home, but the mere thought of what was waiting for me was enough to spoil my good mood, and with that, my mind began to churn. *I have so much to do. I need to do laundry, get groceries, check emails, and then there's my job... What's going to happen now?*

I took a deep breath and chased all these thoughts away. I had a more important task in mind. I must take charge of my life.

Peter noticed my eyes were shut tight and my hands clenched in a fist. "Hey, sweetheart, remember what I said? Everything's going to be okay. The plane has landed safely, and soon we'll be home."

I nodded thinking of my last resolution. *Get my life in order so that we can enjoy our relationship.*

We deplaned and followed our fellow passengers to the customs line. We were lucky the line was short and moved quickly. We used the self-serve terminals and sped through the customs officer booth. With a deep sigh of relief, we were cleared to proceed to collect our luggage in no time at all.

Peter stationed himself strategically in front of the conveyor belt at our designated luggage carousel. I stood back to observe our fellow passengers. I was actually looking for Julia and Scott, but Jen and Ben caught my eye instead.

"Hey, guys, I guess it's back to the real world now, eh?"

"Yup," replied Ben while rolling his eyes.

I turned to Jen, "I guess you guys are anxious to see your son, Eddy?"

"Yes, of course. We're picking up our car, and we're going straight to visit him. We brought him a Roatan rum cake. I hope he doesn't get too drunk on it." Jen smiled at me.

We chatted for a few more minutes when the conveyor belt began circulating the luggage. I looked around searching for Peter and spotted him pulling one of our bags from the luggage carousel.

I quickly said my goodbyes to Jen and Ben and went to catch up with Peter, who was keeping an eye out for our second piece of luggage. On my way I spotted Julia and Scott leaving the baggage claim area. *Shoot, I really wanted to give them my best wishes and say farewell. I guess I can always text them…*I reached Peter just as he was picking up our second piece of luggage from the belt. In a swift arching movement, he deposited the luggage at my feet and said, "Come on sweetheart, let's go home."

"Yes, sir," I said as I pulled the suitcase along the airport floor. Peter was in a hurry, and I could barely keep up with him. About halfway to the exit, I saw Scott speaking to an older gentleman. Peter noticed me hesitating and nudged me, "Come on, darling, we need to grab a taxi before the line gets too long!"

"Wait! I want to say goodbye to Scott and Julia!"

"What again? I thought you already did that!" Peter wanted to get home as soon as possible. That was his sole focus at this point. But I didn't care. I felt it was important to speak to my friends one more time before parting ways.

In any event, Scott was standing not far from the exit doors, so Peter should not be too upset. I walked fast and Peter followed me begrudgingly, a few steps behind.

"Hi, Scott, sorry to interrupt, I just wanted to give you and Julia a proper send off."

"Sure thing, Misty. This is Julia's father."

Julia's father looked like a distinguished businessman. He was wearing a grey suit and a blue tie, which I found a tad odd given that it was the weekend. Julia's father extended his hand and introduced himself.

"Hello, I'm Stephen."

"Nice to meet you sir. I'm Misty, and this is Peter, my boyfriend. Where's Julia?"

"Oh, she's not far. She went to the washroom."

"You know sir, I met Julia at the resort, and I got to know her a little. She is a wonderful girl."

"Thank you, Misty. Indeed, she is a very special girl. She's my daughter, after all."

Without missing a beat, I replied, "And she is very lucky to have a father who will take the time to come to the airport and give his daughter a ride home."

"Please don't embarrass me, Misty. I did what any father would do." Stephen broke into a good healthy laugh.

"And by the way sir, I also met Cheryl at the resort. She too is absolutely wonderful. You are so lucky to have two stunning daughters."

Stephen was no longer laughing and clinched his jaw. His face turned pale like he had seen a ghost. I thought he was going to choke as he swallowed hard a couple of times before he was able to speak again.

"Misty, did I hear you right? You said you met Cheryl?"

"Yes, we all met Cheryl at the resort. I understand that she left Roatan on an earlier flight."

"Misty, it's important for you to understand something about Julia. Julia does not have a sister."

"What do you mean? Cheryl told us that Julia was her sister. Who is she, if she's not Julia's twin sister?"

"What I'm about to tell you may shock you. I don't usually tell this sort of thing to strangers, but I know that you befriended Julia and seem to care for her. It's important for you, Misty, and all of you, to understand one thing about my daughter. Julia is not always herself."

Scott seemed more troubled than shocked about what Stephen had just said.

"What does that mean?" Scott asked, not fully grasping what Stephen was trying to tell us.

"Cheryl exists only in Julia's head."

It took us a while to fully comprehend what Julia's father had just told us. We were dumb-founded. Rendered speechless. We did not know what or whom to believe. Julia's father had just revealed to us something so astonishing, so unexpected, that I had a hard time believing it.

"How can this be possible? I don't under-stand?" I glanced at Peter and Scott, who were standing beside me, looking as stunned as I was.

Peter was the first one to recover from the shock. He asked Stephen the question we all had on our minds. "Was Julia playing us?"

"Not at all. Julia and Cheryl are one person."

"So, when we thought we were speaking to Cheryl, we were actually talking to Julia? Is that what you're telling us?"

"Yes," Stephen replied.

"Wait a minute," I said. "I have a hard time accepting what you just told us. I spent time with her or them, whatever. I really felt that I was speaking to two different people. Cheryl is soft-spoken, and friendly. Julia is more assertive and can be aloof at times. They can't be the same person?"

"They are, believe me. When Julia is under extreme pressure, she changes personality and becomes Cheryl. And when she is in that state, she truly believes that she is Cheryl. She tends to make up her own alternate reality and says things that may be not true. You see, Cheryl is a coping mechanism for Julia. The way her doctor explained it to me is that when she gets emotionally distressed, she reverts to Cheryl's personality because she is totally incapable of dealing with any pain, anguish, fear or any other stressful situation. What the psychologists told me is that Julia has a form of dissociative identity disorder. It sounds like a complicated medical term, but it simply means that she has multiple personalities."

"I can't imagine what it must be like, poor thing," I said.

I could see in Stephen's eyes that he wanted to tell us more. It was like he was carrying a huge burden on his shoulders that he desperately needed to unload. It could not be easy for him to constantly worry about what trouble his daughter could get herself into. I understood his need to talk about it. Being able to share his pain with someone must be a huge relief, I thought.

"You know, Julia is aware of her other personality, but she has no control when it comes out and takes over. Julia created her imaginative sister, Cheryl, shortly after her mother passed away. I tried to help her the best way I knew how. But that was not enough. I had no idea what was going on in her little head. I'm afraid I was not there enough for her when she needed me the most. I encouraged her to have friends, but she preferred to stay home alone in her room. She pretended to have a sister, instead."

Peter, Scott, and I were dumbfounded. Astounded would be a better way to describe how we felt as we listened intently to Julia's father. Stephen had kept his hands buried deep inside his pockets the whole time he spoke to us. I tried to say something but ended up choking on my words. This time it was Scott's turn to finally break the awkward silence. Scott stroked his hair, and figured he might as well say it now.

"Oh my God, I can't believe it! When I was with Julia at the resort, she seemed so normal."

I saw the anguish on Stephen's face after Scott's insensitive remark and the look of disapproval Peter gave him. So, I quickly interjected before Peter had a chance to scold Scott.

"She is a very brave and strong woman, your daughter," I said, projecting as much empathy as I could muster in my voice.

With teary eyes Julia's father looked up at me and nodded slowly.

"Sir, I can't imagine the grief you must have felt losing your wife and how hard it must be for you to have to deal with your daughter's mental condition."

Stephen's eyes welled with tears. "Thank you, thank you, for listening to me. I did not mean to bother you with my troubles. It's just that I'm so relieved to have Julia back home. She has taken off before, you know. There are certain triggers that can cause her to switch personalities. This time I think it was the anniversary of her mother's death. She spontaneously booked a trip to Roatan. She didn't even tell me. I didn't know she had left Canada until she texted me wanting me to pick her up at the airport.

"Again, sir, I can't say enough how sorry I am. Did you know that she nearly drowned?"

"Yes, Misty, she told me in the text message. When I found out that she had flown to Roatan, I immediately thought of her mother. I was so worried that Julia would do something stupid."

"Are you saying that she might have attempted to drown on purpose?"

"To tell you the truth, the thought crossed my mind several times. When I read her text, I knew that something was terribly wrong. You see, Julia's mother drowned while snorkeling in Little French Key. The doctor warned me about Julia. She thinks she can save her mother from drowning if she swims to her and brings her back to safety. In her mind, she can be that twelve-year-old girl again."

I suddenly felt a presence behind me. I turned around and saw Julia watching us from a short distance. She must have known we were talking about her. She hesitated for a few moments unsure of herself and then acknowledged me by waving. No one spoke when she joined our little group. There was a long uncomfortable silence as we all kept staring at each other. Were we embarrassed? I did not think so. Were we lost for words? Absolutely. We were simply too preoccupied to make sense of what we had been told. It was shocking to say the least.

Julia's father rushed to her, and they both held onto each other in a tight embrace. Julia wiped tears from her eyes and smiled at me while grasping tightly onto her father's hand.

Smiling back at her, I said, "Julia, we were just chatting with your father."

"Yeah, I guess you all know now that I am not who you thought I was?" She flipped her hair away from her face, and cast her eyes down.

"What I know is that you have a great father who will take good care of you and some new friends who are here for you when you need us."

Julia hugged me tightly and held on for a long time. I needed it as much as she did. We both had tears in our eyes when she finally let go.

"Thank you all," she said while wiping her tears from her eyes.

Peter and I said our goodbyes and left Stephen, Julia, and Scott behind. About halfway out the door, I stopped to look back. Julia was holding onto her father's hand while chatting with Scott.

"Misty, her father will take good care of her. She'll be fine."

"Oh God, I hope so."

We proceeded to walk outside the terminal looking for a taxi. We stood slightly apart and did not speak to each other while we waited in line for our turn. It was not until we were comfortably seated in the back of the taxi that Peter broke the silence.

"I've never met anyone with multiple personalities. Can someone actually not realize who they are?"

"Yes, Peter, it's a real mental illness, that's not well understood."

"Wow, I can't imagine what that must be like. I mean…to live like that… It must be so scary and difficult. Poor girl."

"I know, Peter. And from what I understand there's no cure. It's confusing and hard for us to understand. But just imagine what it's like for her."

"Yeah, it must be really agonizing. And hard for her father too."

"Yes, I'm sure it's difficult all around, but it sounds like she has a solid support system."

"Listen to you, Misty. You always look for the good side of things, no matter what. You know, if there is one thing I've learned on this trip is that you are the most wonderful person I've ever known. Yes, you tend to worry too much. But that is not necessarily bad. You are the most caring person I know. That's what I love the most about you."

"Thanks, sweetheart. I kind of have firsthand experience with mental illness, don't I?" I gave Peter a telling look.

"Your case is different. You have an anxiety disorder, not multiple personalities."

"I know, but an anxiety disorder is also a form of mental illness which requires attention, medication, and professional help. Most mental health practitioners would tell you that medication and exercise are what you need to manage anxiety disorder. That might be true to an extent. But I happen to believe that you also must have an unshakeable determination to get better in order to conquer your illness. And of course, your love and patience, sweetheart, will also go a long way to help with my recovery. You saw how my anxiety took over on our vacation. I was not taking good care of myself. I'll never let this happen again. I hope it didn't spoil our trip."

"Hey, let's focus on the good times we had on our vacation. How about your birthday celebration at Vintage Pearl? And that day trip to Little French Key, wasn't that amazing?"

"You're right! I had a great time despite it all. And thank you again for an unforgettable birthday, my love."

I rested my head on Peter's shoulder and closed my eyes feeling happy. At last, I felt that Peter was finally getting it. This whole affair with Julia had opened his eyes to the fact that certain minds work differently. That it takes a good level of empathy and sensitivity to live with someone who is afflicted with mental health issues. That patience is paramount. But above all, the will to fight and get better while feeling loved are keys to achieving a strong and satisfying relationship.

There might be a future for us after all.

Our taxi driver drove us home and didn't attempt to strike a conversation with us, sensing perhaps that something special was happening in the back of his car. Little did he know that we had made a major breakthrough in our relationship.

My affliction required patience, understanding, and loving care. Peter was making a real effort to understand me.

I was happy to be home.

CHAPTER 18

"Don't let your struggle become your identity."

–Unknown

few weeks passed, and Peter and I had made the big move. On a sunny Saturday afternoon, we packed our bags and moved in together in a tiny loft high above Humber Bay overlooking Lake Ontario. My anxiety medication had kicked in and, although I was back at the office, I felt much better about myself. It was springtime in Toronto, and the weather was getting warmer. Peter and I spent many nights together cuddling in front of the TV, and things were great between us.

I must confess, though, that I was feeling nervous at first about taking the plunge to live together. Peter had kept pressuring me relentlessly from the time we first landed until a couple of weeks ago, when I finally gave in. With a better understanding of my condition, Peter had assured me living together would be great for both of us. I told him that I'd go ahead on a trial basis, reserving my final decision until I was absolutely certain that it was the right thing for us to do. Roatan had taught me a valuable lesson. *Take it slow.* Peter did not like this "trial" arrangement but relented when he came to terms that it was the only way it was going to work for me.

Back at the office, I found that I could better manage the stress of the daily grind. We had a few months to go before the firm would close its doors. The constant uncertainty of the previous toxic environment had mutated into a kind of acceptance. After all, the end was inevitable. We now knew where we stood, and we could make plans to move forward. I decided to take things one day at a time and accept the clear fact that certain things were beyond my control.

I had become close with some of my coworkers over the years. My little team had become a family. I knew that our paths would cross again for some of us, but it would never be quite the same. We all had our quirks, and we challenged each other at times, but our respect was mutual. There was a certain level of comfort we had reached with each other over the years. A close professional camaraderie had developed among us, and I would make a point of maintaining certain meaningful relationships.

Most of us had been in the business long enough to access a network of contacts who could potentially help us land new opportunities. Some had jobs lined up, and a few people, like me, planned to take some time off. I had a lot to figure out now that I had the time to think clearly. Offers of a severance package had materialized, which would carry me for some time until my next chapter. Perhaps I could persuade Peter to take another trip…

I often thought about our trip to Roatan. It was not just a vacation, it felt more like a journey, a required passage in our lives. Peter and I had grown closer because of it. Indeed, Roatan was a mystical island that had played its magic on us.

I often thought about Julia as well. I hoped she was getting better too. I wanted to reach out to her, but I was not sure it was the right thing to do. I didn't want to make things worse by reminding her of what had happened in Roatan.

One sunny Sunday morning, I was enjoying breakfast alone in the kitchen when I heard a ping on my phone. It was a text message from Julia.

Hi, Misty, It's Julia. How are you doing?

I was pleasantly surprised to hear from her and quickly responded to her text.

Hi, Julia, I am well, thanks. It's so great to hear from you! How are you doing?

I'm much better now, thanks.

Have you heard from Scott?

Yes, we've been on a few dates. He still does not fully grasp why I'm the way I am. He really tries to help the best way he can. How about you and Peter?

It's going great. We moved in together. It took a few adjustments, but things are working out just fine.

Misty, there's something I wanted to tell you for quite some time. You will think that I imagine things, but please trust me about what I'm about to tell you. You're the only person who'll understand. When I was struggling against the current, my life slipping away from me under the water, I heard my mother's voice imploring me to hang on. She said that I should stop worrying so much about her, that she was fine, and it was time for me to take better care of myself. She gave me strength when I needed it the most. And I knew at that moment that I had to move on with my life. I'm still on medication but somehow, everything seems better now that I know my mother is in a good place and will always be looking over me. The shock of losing her was like a wound that would never heal. I often had night-mares about it. I buried myself in my room and cried myself to sleep most nights. I always thought that no one could understand what I was going through. And certainly not my father. He puts on a confident front most of the time and can discuss my condition openly, but he is unable to face up to his own feelings. I don't want to live like that anymore. I now know that I needed to go back to Roatan to stop hiding from myself.

I was so happy to hear that she was feeling better. Julia had made a major breakthrough. It made me realize that something magical had occurred to both of us on that island. *Yes, indeed Roatan was full of magical powers*, I thought to myself. Julia and I had something in common. A shared experience of how it feels to be different. *People want to help but often they can't, simply because they don't understand and don't take the time to learn what is essential for our needs.* But our mental struggles could be managed once in the open, for those who care about us to acknowledge and accept. When Julia reached out to me, I knew I had a friend for life. Someone to lean on. Someone to support. A kindred spirit.

There was so much I wanted to share with Julia. Her text had opened a floodgate of emotions in me. And the important thing was that she had not given up on life. Julia was a fighter.

I liked that about her. I felt as if we could really help one another. Our paths had crossed for a reason.

With teary eyes and trembling lips, I typed two words.

Let's talk.

"We are like islands
in the sea, separate
on the surface
but connected in the deep."

—William James

EPILOGUE

I dare to dream…

*That our story about our relationship's challenges
and struggles will be shared by many readers,
To raise awareness about mental illness and how it
impairs the afflicted
And those who surround them
And to showcase an exotic and beautiful island
In order to inspire future journeys and stories.*

*I dream of Roatan and its breath taking vista.
I picture our book on display in the window of the
little gift shop at Infinity Bay.
I dream of a film with actors and the Roatan people
working together to bring our story to life.*

I hear the ocean calling me in my dream. It's telling me to make my wishes come true.
I'm a believer in the human capacity to overcome the impossible.
I dare to dream.

Misty
April 30, 2024

ABOUT THE AUTHORS

Nancy Kolodzie resides in Toronto and works in the financial service industry. She enjoys spending time with family, friends, travelling, and gardening. Nancy was inspired to tell this story, after a trip to Roatan with her life partner who, at that time, happened to be a writer without a story.

Georges Benay is a former international banker who is now working as a Toronto-based writer and award-winning photographer. He is the author of two novels, *Nomad on the Run* and *the*

Nomad's Premonition and a collection of short stories. His award-winning pictures have been featured in several magazines and book covers.

http://www.amazon.com/author/georgesbenay